CHERRY—
DEADLY DELIGHT

I'm Cherry Delight and I'm good at what I do. No boast, just fact. With revolver or automatic I can put six out of six in a bullseye, or a body. My hair is natural red—hence the Cherry—and a Delight is what I am for people I like, or those I want to destroy. Mostly I want to destroy the Mafia, and that's why I'm top agent for N.Y.M.P.H.O. (otherwise known as the NEW YORK MAFIA PROSECUTION AND HARASSMENT ORGANIZATION). I love sex and I hate the Mob. I break the old guys backs and the young guys hearts—usually with a bullet. I can speak six languages and kill without saying a word.

THE CHERRY DELIGHT SERIES

CHERRY DELIGHT #2

TONG IN CHEEK

GLEN CHASE
(Gardner F. Fox)

First Published in 1973 by Nordon Publications Inc.

First Fiction House Edition January 2021

isbn 9781-64720-209-5

Fiction House Press
www.FictionHousePress.com

Prologue

The three men sat in the darkest booth in the bar and grille, their eyes touching each newcomer as he entered. From time to time their eyes scanned a woman who sat with nyloned legs crossed high to show a stretch of pallid thighflesh, at the long bar behind which the bottles and glasses were reflected in a blue glass mirror.

The men were hard-faced, but neatly dressed. One had a tiny scar running from the corner of his tight mouth to his chin, that gave his not unhandsome face the look of a rough character; he was in his middle thirties, his hair was black, curly, and beginning to bald at the temples. The second man was in his twenties, slim and wiry, with longish hair neatly brushed back, a small moustache covering his upper lip. The third man was big and heavyset, his expensive clothes seemed almost to be bursting at the seams. His dark face was thickly jowled, his flesh coarse.

Their eyes were alert, always moving.

Their hands merely toyed with the drinks before them, three sazeracs they did not touch. Cigarettes glowed between fingers that seemed almost like claws, and a Cinzano ashtray on the booth tabletop was filled with butts of others they had smoked.

"Where in hell is he?" asked the moustached man.

"Easy, Enzo, easy," rumbled the heavyset man.

"You have no nerves, Tommasso."

The bar and grille was quiet in this late afternoon. Soon it would fill with men on their way home from work, stopping in for a quick drink, perhaps to make a pickup of the garishly dressed women who would come here looking for business. At the moment the bar was quiet, a bartender dozed in the sunlight tinting the windows a faint gold.

A shadow darkened the doorway as the door opened.

The woman fussed with a compact, touching a powderpuff to her nose. The three men lifted their drinks now, sipped, the glasses and their hands hiding their faces.

The newcomer looked around him, nodded as if to himself, crossed the tiled floor to a bar chair close to the woman, rested his forearms on the bartop.

"Martini," he said to the bartender. "And see what the lady will have."

She heard his words, smiled and turned toward him, snapping shut the compact. "Why, thanks, mister. That's real nice of you. Off early from work, aren't you?"

"I'm a salesman, my hours are my own."

He moved over a seat, resting easily beside the woman. His eyes touched her blonde hair, studied the push of big breasts bared in a lowcut dress, eyed the slim, shapely nyloned legs he could see to her garterclasps. She gave off an aura of flesh and perfume, her blue eyes were bold, and she let her hand rest idly on the stranger's upper left thigh.

"You looking for action?" she asked softly.

"I'll pay well for the kind of action I like," he said soberly.

Her smile grew wider. "I'm where the action is, honey. And you'd better believe it."

The man nodded, lifted his martini and sipped. The woman flashed him a flirtatious glance out of mascaraed eyes, raised her manhattan. She let her tongue dip into the cocktail a moment, catlike, before she put the glass to her mouth.

The man smiled. "We'll get along," he said. He hesitated a moment, then asked very softly, "You bring it with you?"

She whispered, "Don't talk here, honey. But—I always bring it with me."

They talked about the weather, baseball and the latest government scandal until they had finished their drinks. The man slid a five dollar bill toward the bartender, told him to keep the change, and turned his head to stare at the stockinged legs of the woman as she swung in his direction and parted them slightly to slide off the bar stool.

He saw dark inside of her thighs, the black nylons, the wink of light on a garterclasp. As the woman went out before him, his eyes touched her wobbling buttocks, unfettered under the thin print dress she wore. It was minilength and showed off her ripely curved legs to the middle of her thighs. The man felt his breath come more quickly, touched his lips with his tongue, and went out into the sunlight with her. On the sidewalk, she put her arm around his. An onlooker might have taken them for man and wife.

The three men in the booth sat there, unmoving.

"Give them time," said Tommasso Ribaldo.

"An hour, she said," growled the man with the scar on his face.

The smallest of the three chuckled. "Tina wants her screwin', Cesare. It was part of the deal."

Cesare Iannotto shrugged, stared into his untouched sazerac.

The man and woman moved between the passersby, oblivious to them. The man was only too conscious of the brush of her ungirdled hip, the touch of a soft thigh against his own. He reminded himself that he was here on business, the woman was to hand over certain papers that his organization wanted. Still, there was no law saying that he shouldn't have a little fun at the same time.

When they came to an apartment house two blocks away, the woman murmured out of the corner of her mouth, "Let me go first. You come right up to three bee."

His instincts clamored with suspicion. He said thightly, "I'd rather go up with you, sweets. That way, there won't be anybody there waiting for me, or if there is, you'll be in the line of fire, too."

"Oh! I never thought of that. I was going to slip into something comfortable and offer you a drink and maybe even something more if you're nice."

"Let me watch," he told her.

"I'd like that," she nodded happily. "You and I are going to get along fine."

Then they were in the cool lobby, moving toward an elevator. The woman punched a stud marked 3. The man put his arm about her middle, brought her soft body in against his own. She could feel how hard he was with her upper thigh: she smiled lazily and rubbed herself against it.

"You're kind of hard up, aren't you?" she breathed.

"Hard but not hard up," he chuckled.

"You made a funny. I like a man with a sense of humor."

The carpeting was worn here and there but the

hallway was clean, and when the woman opened the door of her apartment, one raking glance told the man that the place was not only empty, but clean. He touched the butt of the Colt revolver in his shoulder holster, loosened it.

He walked through the living room with its curved sofa and coffee table, the two easy chairs and little bar, toward the bedroom. His hand was on the Colt as he looked a quick look inside the bedroom, noting the queen-size bed, the chintz drapes and the vanity table with the chintz-hung bench. He went from the bedroom to the bathroom, checked it, then peered into the tiny kitchenette.

When he came back to the living room, the woman asked with a lift of her plucked blond brows, "Satisfied?"

He nodded, moved toward the door, checked the lock. He said, "You ought to have a chain, things be-ing what they are these days."

"I've thought about it. I guess I'm just lazy, I keep putting things off. You want another martini?"

She took a bottle of Tanqueray gin and poured, reached for a Tribuno bottle. She added ice, brought the drink to him.

"You want to look at the papers first—or at me?"

He smiled, sipped. "The papers first. I want to check them. Then we can have the whole day and the night." He hesitated, added, "I'm willing to pay for your services."

"It's well covered by the money. You did bring the cash, didn't you?"

He reached into his hip pocket, brought out a wallet. He took out five one thousand dollars bills, fanned them. The woman stared at them with greed in her eyes, licked her full mouth.

"I'll get the papers," she nodded.

He seated himself in an easy chair, put the cocktail glass within reach. When she brought him the envelope, he said, "My name's Bill. We ought at least to be on a first name basis."

"I'm Tina."

He scanned the papers, noting the names and addresses on them. He handed the thousand dollar bills to Tina, slipped the papers back inside the envelope and pushed the envelope inside his coat jacket so that it lay flat beside his notebook.

Tina pulled out a drawer of a small writing desk, placed the money inside a diary, then turned to the man. Her hands went to the zipper on the back of her flowered print and ran it down. She smiled lazily, looking at him.

"Why not get comfy yourself, Bill?"

He rose, slid out of his jacket, tossing it across the chair, then unbuckled his shoulder holster harness. By the time this was off, the woman was sliding the dress down her arms, showing off her rounded shoulders and the upper slopes of big breasts barely contained by the C cups of her black lace Olga bra.

Her breasts shook loosely as she came forward a few steps toward the man.

Her eyes were glazing, he saw, there was the look of rut heat in them. He had already guessed that she was a hooker in the employ of the Mafia, he knew she was Big Tommy's girl friend; that was how she was able to get the list of names and addresses for which his organization was paying the five grand. She was one dame who liked her work, who looked forward to each encounter with a man.

Like now. There was heat in her eyes, in the quivering of her breastflesh, in the gentle side to side movement of her hips. He'd bet she was wet between her legs, too, just at the idea of taking his yard into her. That was all right with him; he'd been without a dame for a long time, now. He was just as eager as she.

The dress was at her middle, she was bending over, letting her breasts hang more fully into the Olga bra cups as she pushed the dress down. The shaking of those lush orbs was getting to him. His mouth was dry, it was hard to swallow, and his penis was like a bar of steel.

Almost of their own will, his hands lifted to her breasts. He cradled their brassiered fullness on his palms, he shook them up and down as the woman paused in her undressing to smile up at him.

"You a titty man?" she whispered.

"I like everything about you, Tina. Everything!"

She crooned in her throat, gave her dress a shove. It slid past bare hips framed in the black lace garterbelt, past her slightly pouching belly and the black hairs clustering so thickly between her plump upper thighs. She felt his fingers sliding into the brassiere, lifting out her breast.

He bent the bra cups under her breasts so that they stood out in bold detail, the red nipples stiff and jutting. She straightened slowly, wearing only garterbelt and black nylons, the highheeled shoes, and the bulging brassiere.

Tina cupped his face with her hands, drew his head down. "Go ahead, you want to. I like it, a man with his mouth on my nipples."

He drew them in, hungrily.

The afternoon was hushed, the sound of traffic beyond the apartment windows muted. The woman stood with her head backflung, lower lip between her teeth. The man had put his palms on her naked sides, was sliding them up and down, below her garterbelt to the roundings of her hips and along her thighs, then upward, even as his mouth sucked gently on the nipple it held.

"Oh my God," she whimpered, pushing her hips forward. "You're teasing me, Bill. I love to be t-teased, but you're getting me ho-hot. Real hot!"

"The way I want you," he whispered to the erect red nipple between his lips. "I want you so hot you'll let me do whatever I want!"

"As long as you don't hurt me, I don't care what you do, honey. I like it all sorts of ways."

"Hurting isn't my bag. I just want to love the hell out of you."

"Then come on, do it,"

She caught his head, lifted it so her wide wet mouth could close on his. She pushed her tongue into his mouth, licked his tongue, his teeth. His hands were on her soft white buttocks, squeezing them, holding her belly against his so that she could feel the length and stiffness of his yard.

Now her hands came into play, sliding down between them, gripping his belt and loosening the buckle, sliding down his fly. Her thumbs went to his pants, caught his jockey shorts, pushed them downward.

He stood naked against her, his male flesh could feel the brush of her soft pubic hairs against his penis, and the touching of her muscled belly against his. Her arms came about him, holding him as she writhed herself against his own nakedness. Their lips feasted, their tongues played together, the breath of each came short and shallow.

The woman began to walk backward, very slowly, bringing him with her, step by step, increasing his desire by the motion of her legs, the caresses of her bushy mons veneris and belly. She took away her mouth from his lips, transferred it to his shoulders where she bit gently.

His hands were under her breasts, shaking them, sliding fingers over the hardening fullness of their mounds. His forefingers and thumbs caught her nipples, rotated them, tugged them outward even as they walked.

To her bedroom door she brought him, then whirled and moved away from him slowly, letting him look at her stockinged legs, the backs of her pale thighs and the quivering buttocks—everything he wanted.

She was a woman, warm and soft, ready to bed him down, and his eyeballs roamed over her nudity, feasting on her pink buttocks as she bent over the bed to draw back the chintz bedspread. He could see the black crotch hairs between her upper thighs as she leaned, and his heart thudded with sexual excitement.

He crossed to the bed, dropped to his knees behind her, caught her hips and began kissing her soft buttocks, the soft female flesh under his face. He rubbed his flushed cheeks against her behind, smelling the muskiness of her moist genitals, the perfume with which she had touched them, earlier in the day.

She laughed throatily, let her hips move backward, fondling his face with her soft asscheeks. "I love that, Bill. A real lover—a real man—enjoys every part of a woman."

Now her left leg lifted so she could kneel on the edge of the bed and the man kissed her inner thigh, his eyes darting to her soft bush.

The woman moved onto the bed, turned on her back and raised her nyloned legs. Her glazed eyes stared at his hairy loins, saw the readiness of his male spear.

"Put it in me, Bill. Put it in deep."

With a soft cry he came between her upraised thighs, watched as she stretched out a hand to catch hold of him, to hold his shaft steady to his red target as he lunged. He sank deep, deep, and he cried out, head going back in the primitive lust that shook his body.

Forgotten for the moment were the papers inside his jacket pocket, his Colt revolver in its shoulder holster—the five thousand dollars he had paid this woman. All that counted now was his flesh in her flesh, hard and aching, and the moist grip of her body that held him.

Her hips moved gently, squirming.

Tina Carfacci was panting herself, sobbing to the thrustings of his male shaft, to the dig of its velvety steel against her vaginal walls. She too had forgotten the reason for meeting this man and the fact that three men were even now leaving the bar and grille to kill him. Her bare arms came up to wrap about his body, to hold him close.

Their bared hips rose and fell. . . .

On the sidewalk outside the apartment house, Enzo Fuselli, Cesare Iannotto and Tommasso Ribaldo walked with slow strides, neither lazing along nor hurrying. They moved as do men on a mission, without pausing to do more than watch for traffic as they came to a street intersection or observe with careful eyes the fact that no police squad cars were in sight.

The heavyset man said, "We go right in, to the elevator. We don't stop to do anything else. It's like we lived there, understand?"

"Okay," Enzo Fuselli said.

"We do the hit, then we leave for China."

They walked on, their footfalls soft, almost silent.

At the apartment house entrance their eyes flashed across the lobby, found it empty. Then they proceeded leisurely to the open elevator door. They went in, the man with the scar on his face touched a finger to the third floor button. The elevator car door slid shut, the car began its rise.

They stepped out of the elevator, moved along the corridor. Big Tommy reached into his trouser pocket for a key ring. He stopped at 3B, looked up and down the hall, then inserted the key into the lock. Gently, he turned it.

The sounds of sex came from the bedroom as they came into the apartment. Cesare Iannotto grinned. He opened his month but closed it when Tommasso Ribaldo looked at him.

Enzo Fuselli drew an automatic from his shoulder holster, got a silencer from his jacket pocket, fitted it on. The others watched him, and then they too, readied their weapons for the kill.

Tommasso Ribaldo nodded, and the man with the small moustache went first, the scarfaced man at his heels, Big Tommy in the rear. They moved like shadows across the room, paused a moment, listening to the woman crying out and the man's rough grunting, and then Enzo Fuselli stepped into the doorway. The woman saw him and her eyes grew large.

Her hands came up to the man's shoulders, pushed him back, crying out in alarm. Bill Tomkins caught her terror, reacted to it by flinging himself from her body, sliding to the edge of the bed, rolling off it.

While he crouched there, staring at them, Enzo Fuselli pulled the trigger. The popping sound was loud in the room, but the three men knew it would not be heard beyond its walls. A tiny black spot appeared in Bill Tomkin's naked chest. His eyes widened, his mouth opened.

Cesare Iannotto fired. So did Big Tommy.

Tomkins was dead on his naked feet, the second and third bullets merely pushed him backward so that he sprawled against the base of the far wall, limp and lifeless. There was a faint silence in the room in which only the woman's soft sob made any sound.

Big Tommy ran his eyes over her soft body,

studying the creased bellyflesh, the slightly sagging breasts, the heavy thighs. He grinned coldly, raised his silencer-fitted, automatic and sighted along its barrel.

Tina yelled, "Hey! What in hell do you think you're doing?"

"Just practising, kiddo." He lowered the gun.

Enzo Fuselli asked, "Where's the papers?"

"In—in his coat pocket."

"Go get 'em, Cesare."

The scarred man whirled, moved quickly into the other room. An instant later he called, "Got 'em."

Tommasso Ribaldo asked, "Where's the five grand?"

Careless of her nudity, Tina slid to the edge of the bed, her face sullen. "I was told I got to keep the money."

"You were told wrong. Where is it?"

"In my desk, inside my diary."

"Get it, Enzo."

Seconds later, the man with the moustache called out, "Okay."

Again Big Tommy raised his gun. He zeroed its sight in on the heavy, sagging breasts, aimed between them. The woman watched him, holding her breath.

"Stop kidding, Tommy," she whispered.

He squeezed the trigger.

The woman went backward as though a giant

hand had struck her. She sprawled in death, arms flung wide, blood beginning its ooze from beneath her breasts. Her thighs were a little apart, showing the red genital gash, the black hairs of her bush.

"Stupid bitch," growled the heavyset man.

He walked across the bedroom carpet, stared at the dead man, then turned to study the woman. He nodded once, satisfied. Slowly he undid the silencer, put it in a pocket. He slid the automatic into his shoulder holster.

Then he walked into the living room.

"Got everything—papers, the money?" he asked.

Fuselli nodded.

Iannotto chuckled, held up a slim notebook in tooled leather. "There's an extra dividend, Tommasso. His notebook with all kinds of stuff written in it."

"Bring it along, might be interesting. Let's go."

Tommasso Ribaldo waited while they put their guns away.

Chapter One

I paused in front of the mirror to study my girl-girl body, naked except for a pair of black bikini panties and sheer nylon negligee. I had a date tonight with Mark Condon, who is my contact man in the Mafia-fighting group known as the New York Mafia Prosecution and Harrassment Organization, more commonly called N.Y.M.P.H.O. As my eyes assessed my contours, I decided Mark Condon was going to flip over what I was looking at, what he'd look at later.

My name is Cherry Delight. I'm a redhead, a girl operative of N.Y.M.P.H.O., and right then I was between assignments, which meant I could live life as life was meant to be lived. Mark Condon would take me to a Broadway musical for which he had third row tickets, and after that we would dine at the Russian Tea Room on *nalistniki* and champagne, with an

Irish Coffee to top it off.

My eyes touched the bed where my Marc Bohan see-through, midi-length chiffon evening gown was waiting to be slithered into; it would take but one second to doff the negligee and put the gown on, and I wanted Mark Condon to see me as I was.

The doorbell rang.

I took one last peek at myself, nodded approvingly and ran for the door, holding the negligee around my mostly bare curves. I opened the door. Mark Condon was in the hall with a scowl on his face.

The scowl should have warned me, but I was so happy to see him I forgot for the nonce that he and I worked together. "Come on in," I carolled, and swung the door wide.

He got a good look at my bare breasts under black nylon and my indented bellybutton with all my bare legs showing. His eyes got wide, he whistled soundlessly.

"Hey, wow," he breathed.

"Don't just stand there, come on in."

"It's all wasted, Cherry," he muttered, doing what I asked.

"What's all wasted?" I wanted to know, closing the door behind him.

His hand made a motion in the air. "The girlish goodies are wasted—for now. We have a job to do. The Mafia just got Bill Tomkins."

"Ohhhh, *no!*"

I had liked Bill Tomkins, he was a swell guy, a damn good agent. "How'd it happen?" I asked as Mark sat on the edge of a loveseat, elbows on his knees, hunched forward.

"He was after a list of all the Mafia members. A woman named Tina Carfacci had promised to furnish him with that list in exchange for five thousand dollars. Cheap at any price. Even his life if he got it. But he didn't get it."

"Bill apparently kept his date with her, because both he and she were found dead in her apartment early this morning. The N.Y.M.P.H.O. boys staged a raid because Bill hadn't reported back and we knew where he was going. It wasn't at all like Bill not to report, even by telephone. He always kept in touch.

"The boys found them both naked in the bedroom. He'd been shot with three different thirty-eight calibre bullets—probably the automatics were equipped with silencers, nobody heard any shooting —and she had one slug right through her chest.

"The papers weren't in the apartment. Neither was the five grand."

I felt bad, but I kept it silent.

Then I said softly, "They're afraid somebody would get to her, make her talk. That's why they killed her. The bastards even took the money!"

"There's more than that."

My red eyebrows, carefully plucked to thin lines,

lifted in surprise. "More? How could there be more? Sounds as if someone wrote finish to a great guy, and nothing else."

Mark smiled, his eyes on my bare legs, tracing them with his stare all the way up to where my bikini briefs held in my red pubic bush. He licked his lips, then remembered why he was there.

"Tomkins had done a lot of work on the local Mafia. He made friends with some of their buttons, the muscle-men. A couple of them talked, you know how they brag on booze. Seems the Mafia is moving in on China. Red China, I mean."

"You've got to be kidding!"

"Doesn't seem to make sense, does it? But look at it this way. Ever since the President went to have his talks with Mao-Tse-tung and Chou En-lai, there has been talk of opening trade relations and establishing business connections between Red China and us."

I opened my mouth and gasped.

When I got my breath back I said, "You think the Mafia wants to cut in on those trade agreements! Come off it, Mark."

"Will you wait? Just let me talk." He hesitated, then asked, "Do you know anything about the Chinese tongs that used to flourish in San Francisco and other parts of California early in this century?"

I said I knew something about them.

"Then let me explain." Mark Condon tends to get a little schoolteacherish at times. This was one of the times, so I crossed my bare legs and sank back deeper into my easychair.

"The first tongs began in the gold fields of California just about when the Civil War started, though there's no apparent connection. One was named the Hop Sing, the other was the Suey Sing. They were started to help fellow Chinamen because coolie labor was cheap in those days and the Chinese were despised. Time passed and the tongs turned into gangs.

"They maintained opium dens, they controlled gambling, they established houses of prostitution. And they made money. The different tongs weren't satisfied with this—by now they had formed a sort of yellow underworld in San Francisco—they wanted more. They began to encroach on each other's territories, the same way the Mafia did in the twenties in Chicago and New York, during Prohibition days.

"There's quite a parallel, if you make a study of it, between the tongs and the Mafia. The only difference—the color of their skins.

"Anyhow, the tongs began a struggle for control among themselves. The Hop Sings fought with the Suey Sings, their hatchetmen struck again and again. One of their biggest battles was fought at Waverly Place in Chinatown between the Suey Sings and the Kwong Dock tong. The *bow how doys*—the fighting men of the tongs, their salaried soldiers—met in a grudge fight. Before the police broke it up, at least nine of the *bow how doys* had been seriously wounded.

"But one of the Kwong Docks, the man who had started the war, actually, by killing a member of the Suey Sing tong over a girl, fled to China when the Suey Sing hatchetman started to hunt him down. His name was Ming Long.

"Keep his name in mind," Condon told me.

"That was the first of the tong wars that stretched across the entire last quarter of the nineteenth century. The tongs were very powerful, they were rich, they controlled a lot of powerful interests. One member of the Sum Yap tong, a man named Fung Jing Toy, became absolute master of his little world during that time, with the help of political powers whom he bribed.

"He would rat on fellow vice lords in Chinatown, have the police raid them and shut them down, then reopen the gambling and opium dens, the brothels, with his Sum Yop tong in complete control, untouched by the police. He really made himself king of Chinatown, there's no doubt about it."

Mark was staring at me oddly, so when I glanced down at myself I saw that my negligee had opened and both my generous bare breasts were staring back at him with their brown nipples. I smiled and closed the black nylon, though it didn't really hide very much.

Mark sighed, said, "When Fung Jing Toy got too big for his britches and overreached himself—remember, every tong except his own had a grudge against him and his methods, because he robbed from them all, impartially—they put a price of three thousand dollars on his head. A sum like that would have let his killer go back to China and live like a king.

"They caught up to him in a barber shop in 1897. Funny thing how barber shops figure so much in gangland killings, isn't it? That's where Albert Anastasia got his, in a barber shop, in 1957.

"Somebody named Lem Jung shot the boss tong chief five times in the spine, and that blew the lid off the pot. The other tongs began exterminating the *bow how doy* hatchetmen of the Sum Yops until the Emperor of China himself called a halt to the killing.

"He threatened to put their families—those still in China—in jail if any more Sum Yop hatchetmen were murdered. None were."

Condon said: "Now let's go back to Ming Long."

I chimed in to show I had been paying attention, "He was the man who started the whole thing," by cleaving the skull of a rival tong member over a girl."

"Right. Now back in China, Ming Long figured he had a good thing going. At that time there were no tongs in China. But Ming Long took care of that, he started his own tong and did pretty well for a while.

We weren't sure just what did happen in China, it was still pretty much a closed nation. But we do know he started a tong and other tongs were formed.

"Since then, they've dropped out of sight. Nobody hears a thing about them. But now—even since the resumption of relations between Red China and the United States, there have been stirrings behind the bamboo curtain.

"Overtures have been made to the Mafia by the secret tongs."

I leaned forward, rested my hands on my thighs. This made my breasts swing outward, my nipples nuzzling a path into the lamplight. Mark eyed them hungrily, which I was happy to see.

"You mean to tell me Bill Tomkins learned all this?"

Mark waved a hand. "He learned some of it, especially the bit about the tongs contacting the Mafia. It was in his notes that we found in his apartment. Apparently he was about to write up a report of all this, but he was killed instead."

I'm no mind-reader, but I knew what Mark Condon was about to say. So I said it for him. "So now the organization wants to know more about this Mafia-tong link-up, and I'm the fall guy chosen for the job."

Mark looked embarrassed. He is a big guy, lean and wiry and wears clothes as perfectly as a men's store dummy. He was positively mouth-watering in a Paul Wattenburg chalk-striped worsted with a Hathaway satin-striped shirt and an Oleg Cassini silk tie. Mark Condon likes clothes, so do I. It's one reason we get along so well together.

"Something like that, yes. We have feelers out, we're trying to learn where the three killers went."

"Three killers?"

"Didn't I say that three different guns had fired the bullets into Bill? Our ballistics department has been working overtime. No killer, Mafia or otherwise, normally carries three different guns to do a job. So we have to believe three separate men were involved. And as I said, one of the men who shot Bill also killed the woman."

I frowned. "But where does China come in?"

"We think they'll head for China—Red China—the way Ming Long did a hundred years ago when the heat was on in San Francisco. Tomkins said in his diary that some of them would go there to set up some sort of deal with the tongs. The Coordinator, our bossman, figures the three killers are going to be sent as envoys. It serves a double purpose, it gets them out of the country and it lets them make the contacts."

"I think the boss is just guessing."

Mark shrugged. "Maybe he is. Even so, he's got a pretty high average on those educated guesses he makes. There could be more information in Bill's diary than the Coordinator's letting on. He's working very closely with the police department and the F.B.I. on this. The President, I understand, doesn't want his mission to China to go up in smoke. It could if word got out that American mobsters were joining with Red Chinese mobsters to muscle in on all those nice new trade agreements."

I uncrossed my bare legs. "Makes sense, Mark. The only trouble is, I'm going to be chasing three ghosts in silk suits when it comes to those Mafia killers. I don't know them or what they look like."

"Our men are watching the air terminals. Taking pictures of all suspicious characters. Some of the boys know the hit men for the mob. They're along to make any identifications that may be needed."

I looked him in the eye. "What do we do now?"

Mark grinned, "I gave away the tickets to the show, figuring we wouldn't need them, but there's no reason why we can't go eat *nilistniki* and drink Irish coffee, is there?"

I hopped to my feet, ran for the bedroom. A second or two later I was letting the Marc Bohan evening gown slide down my shapely curves. I snatched up a mink stole and my Coblentz evening bag and made my grand entrance for Mark Condon to admire and whistle at. I beamed as his eyes ran up and down my bod, and got that want-you look.

"We'll have an early evening," I smiled, leading the way toward the door.

"Early to bed," he said, smiling like a cartoon wolf.

Sometimes I think Mark has a dirty mind. But I love it, because he does what he thinks. At times he does. I wasn't sure whether this night was going to be one of the titillating times or not. It kept me on my toes, so to speak.

The *nilistniki* was absolutely super. That dish of ground sirloin steak, mixed with onions, eggs, peppers, dill and other varied ingredients, when served on unsweetened crepes and baked, with the right sauces added, is mouth-watering indeed. Mark and I feasted unashamedly. We drank champagne and then the Irish coffee.

We didn't hurry, we enjoyed ourselves, we made small talk and flirted with each other. I like Chinese food but not all the time. Like not for breakfast. There would be no *nilistniki* in Peking or Shanghai. I had to pamper my taste buds while I could.

We came out of the restaurant and Mark suggested a walk.

The moon was a big silver plate overhead; the night sky was blue velvet. The air was warm, with a hint of coming summer. The breeze that swept along the street was soft and pleasant. I hooked an arm through Mark's and we marched.

Mark Condon is a smoothie. I guess he knows as well as anybody that a big silvery moon in the night sky and a reasonably warm evening will do things to a girl who has partaken of *nilistniki* and champagne and Irish coffee.

He seemed to know what it would do to me. Because he pulled me into a dark street front after a couple of blocks and wrapped his arms around me and kissed me as I hadn't been kissed for too long. I let my thighs and belly tell him what I wanted, and found him ready for a wrestle.

Now I am a member of the Femmes Fatales, a branch of N.Y.M.P.H.O. which consists of very attractive, loveable girls whose job is that of call girl and seductress, sometime killer and general all-around sex symbol. When I am working, I usually get more than my fair share of loving. It's part of the job, but at in-between times, like now, a warm and affectionate nature like mine needs something more than stand-up kisses.

So I whispered, "It's still early, Mark."

"Did I tell you how gorgeous you are in that black nylon negligee?"

"No, but you could start, right about now."

"I like an instant replay of the same, Cherry."

"Not here, Mark."

"You have a great bedroom. It's made for loving."

"Like its owner."

Silly talk, but effective, since Mark had his hand on my thigh and was sliding it around over my belly to my pubes and then up to my breasts, unbrassiered behind the bodice panels of the see-through gown. The material of the gown was thin, so it was almost as if he were caressing my skin. This made the rapping that much more amorous.

"We're wasting time," he panted after a few minutes.

"I thought you'd never ask," I giggled.

We were in no condition to do much walking, so Mark hailed a passing cab which would bring us to my pad on East Seventy-third Street in very short order. Inside the cab, Mark managed to get a hand under my evening gown and run it up my inner thighs. China be damned—all I knew was that I might have to do without the attentions of a lover boy like Mark Condon for quite some time. I let my legs fall apart and scrunched down a little in the taxi seat.

Mark has very deft hands for a big guy. They were like feathers crawling along my inner thighs, right up to my love nest where the red hairs clustered. His fingertips made such gentle love to me, I floated in a love haze all the way to the apartment building.

We slid out of the cab, Mark paid the fare and caught my arm to hurry me into the apartment lobby. My eyes were a little blurred, but I could see well enough to notice two men standing near the lobby, eyeing us with a sharp interest that drew my attention.

I thought nothing of it, though I should have

known better. I was too interested in Mark Condon, his hand stroking my rounded hip through the thin stuff of my evening gown. Maybe my N.Y.M.P.H.O. bosses trained me better than they knew, because I never really relax my guard, even when my love zones are clamoring for relief.

I saw the two men reach into their jackets.

Nobody has to tell me that male characters who carry rods keep them in shoulder holsters on their left side, beneath their jackets. Sure, sure. Maybe they were reaching for cigarettes. But their faces, cold and hard, without pity, added to my instinct for self-preservation.

I grabbed Mark and shoved him just as the guns came out. He let out a yelp and lost his balance, falling with me on top of him. The guns were naked, fingers were curling around the triggers. My own hand was out of sight, reaching into Mark's shoulder holster.

Their thirty-eights made loud sounds in the city night.

Two bullets nicked the sidewalk.

I had Mark's service gun in my hands, whirled and put all my fingers around it to hold it steady. The buttons looked surprised, I guess they didn't figure me for any aggressive acts.

I sighted quickly. My finger squeezed.

The gun bucked in my hand.

I have some sharpshooter medals—revolver or

automatic—tucked away under a pair of frilly panties in my pad. And when I go into action, my blood turns to ice water.

I was more than slightly mad at these musclemen for the Mafia. Here I was, all lathered up in the crotch for a little bed work with lover boy and these gunsels had to spoil it all.

A dark hole leaped to life in the chest of the smaller man. He opened his mouth and his eyes got wide in surprise. Then he started to fall. My gun moved a fraction to the right where the other hit man was trying to zero in on my girl-girl flesh with a .38 calibre bullet. I got mine off first.

He went back on his heels and his right arm dropped. He fell to the pavement and lay there. Beside me, Mark Condon was cursing."

"Hit men, honey," I told him. "Somebody must have given them the contract on you. Maybe on us both."

"Impossible," he breathed.

"Oh, yeah? You didn't hear the shots?" He made it to his feet, yanked me up and we went to look at the two dead men. By this time, people were running toward us along the sidewalk.

"Get the police," Mark snapped.

I ran for the apartment lobby, grabbed the elevator and made it to my rooms. I dialed the police, told them what had happened, that a N.Y.M.P.H.O. agent had done the shooting, that another

N.Y.M.P.H.O. agent was waiting with the bodies. Then I called my own headquarters.

An all-night operator put me through to the Co-ordinator.

The N.Y.M.P.H.O. Coordinator is a tall, lean man with a British accent, greying black hair and he's rather handsome. His Oxbridge voice told me to stay where I was. He'd be over directly to talk to Mark and the homicide men.

"And," he added softly, "That was nice work, Cherry. I'm proud of you and Mark ought to be damn grateful."

"I hope he shows it," I muttered.

A chuckle was my answer, before he hung up.

I paced around my pad like a hungry tigress walking the jungle paths. What was happening down below on the sidewalk? Would I still be going to China? Had someone or something let the cat out of the N.Y.M.P.H.O. bag, so that the Family knew I was headed for the Chinese People's Republic? It seemed hard to believe, but two dead men were lying on the sidewalk.

Eventually, there was a knock on the door.

It was Mark and a beefy young inspector from the Homicide Squad. I told the story exactly as it happened. Mark had a funny look on his face all the time, and it finally dawned on me that this was a kind of put-down for him. After all, he was the male and it was up to him to protect me. Women's Lib would love this little news item, I guessed.

Inspector Adams—Clinton Adams, to be pre-cise—made some notes, then stood up, folding his notebook and putting it back into his jacket pocket. "That'll be about all, Miss Delight. I can make my reports now, and you can forget about this trouble. We'll handle it with your Coordinator."

He was gone and Mark and I were alone.

"Go ahead, Mark. Say it."

"Say what?" he asked smoothly.

"Tell me I took the play away from you. It was what you were thinking while I was talking to the In-spector."

He grinned faintly. "Well, I was annoyed at not discovering those two buttons myself. It doesn't put me in too good a light, does it? The main thing is, you saved both our lives. I'm grateful, I mean it."

"Oh, come off it."

He took a couple of steps and put his arms around me, holding me close. His mouth came down on mine and his hands slid to my buttocks.

After a time he said softly, "You see? I wouldn't be here now doing this to you if you hadn't been so quick down there on the sidewalk. That's one reason why I'm so damn grateful."

My arms were around his neck, my middle mov-ing lazily back and forth against his front. "Well, when you put it that way. . . ."

We kissed some more. I was all set to go into the

slipping-into-something-more-comfortable routine when there was another knock on the door. It was the Coordinator. Maybe he saw the lipstick on Mark's mouth and maybe he didn't. All he did was smile at us and sit the easy chair I gestured him into.

"Why do you think those men were after you, Mark?"

Mark said, "I haven't the faintest."

"I have a theory," I muttered.

They looked at me in surprise, Avery King, the Coordinator, with his British eyebrows raised. "What theory is that, Cherry?"

"Well, Mark is—was Bill Tomkins' contact man, as well as mine. It may be that Bill had some notes in his pocket when he was killed. The hit men took those notes along with the list of names Bill was paying five grand to get. They might have found Mark's name and decided to play safe by rubbing him out, too."

The two men stared at each other. Finally Avery King said in his veddy cultured, veddy English way of speaking, "It makes sense. I can't account for it, otherwise." He glanced at me, asked. "Were they after you, too? Did it seem that way?"

"Not until I started spraying bullets at them."

"That's what I wanted to know. If they suspected you were going to Red China after the men who killed Tomkins, then I'd have to call off your trip."

I waited while he frowned. He went on, I think

that what happened tonight was the Mafia's way of saying they'd finish any war we started. Well, they've made their try and failed.

"They may try again. That means you're a marked man, Condon. Do lay low for a while. Cherry, you keep to your schedule, the flight from Kennedy tomorrow, all the way to Hong Kong with the necessary stopovers.

"Has Mark briefed you, yet?" the Coordinator asked.

Mark looked embarrassed. "Not completely. We were coming up here to talk business when those buttons showed."

Avery King smiled faintly. "Good. Then I'll leave you two alone so you can—ah—discuss business matters before Cherry goes to sleep."

His grey eyes twinkled, but he didn't say a word, the doll. He knew what was going to happen when we finished talking about N.Y.M.P.H.O. business. He gestured me away when I tried to walk him to the door. It closed behind him; I chained it.

Mark was saying, as I turned and moved toward him, "Let's get the business end of it out of the way, Cherry. I have your flight tickets, your sealed instructions, your passport." He took them out of his inside jacket pocket, placed them on my Bruno Mathesson coffee table.

My hand was at the strap of my evening gown. I slid it down slowly in the manner of a strip teaser.

Mark glanced from the papers up at me, and never looked away again. I lowered the other strap, caught both of them in my hands. I did a little shimmy. Mark licked his lips, staring at the upper swells of my breasts that had begun to shake loosely in time with my movements.

"I really ought to have some music," I hinted.

He bounded up and practically ran toward my Harman-Kardon stereo set. In a moment there was the proper music for a girl to strip by, and no wonder, because I'd placed the record there myself, earlier in the evening. I moved around the room with swinging haunches, turned and lowered the upper part of my evening gown so my breasts came out into the light.

I have good breasts, they are big and heavy but very upright, with large brown nipples. Now my nipples were big and extended. It always gets me hot when I bare my body for an adoring male. My hands came up under my breasts, lifted them. I smiled at Mark and gave each titty a milk shake.

"Jeez," he breathed.

"You too," I whispered, and Mark started to undress.

He didn't make a production out of it the way I did. He just undid his tie and threw it, tossed his jacket and then his shirt; in a moment was down to his jockey shorts. He was as excited as hell; his penis stood proudly, hardly contained by the webbed shorts.

I was bare to my slender middle, my navel was winking at him as I started pushing the Marc Bohan gown down further off my body. The more down it went, the more up he came, if I may be permitted a bit of Amish patois. When my red pubic bush came into view below my black and red lace garterbelt, I thought honestly he'd tear the shorts.

The gown pooled at my feet. Ordinarily, I treat a Marc Bohan creation with a little more respect, but Mark seemed in such need. I walked right up to him and let my mostly nude body do the talking.

His erection went between my thighs. I closed them gently, holding him fast. Mark was glassy-eyed, and breathing hard. He was a real doll.

My arms went around his neck, my breasts to his somewhat hairy chest; my lips fastened on his mouth. He put his hands on my smooth shoulders and ran them all the way down to my behind. Mark likes my buttocks, he says they are big white moons of quivering delight, the rascal. His palms and fingers slid over them lazily.

My thighs tightened and loosed on his penishead. Mark groaned.

I said to his tongue: it was licking my lips, "See? You wouldn't be doing this if it weren't for me. Aren't you glad you're alive, darling?"

"Yeah," he grinned, pushing his hips forward. "We have to make this last for quite some time.

You'll be in China and I'll be here, dodging the hit boys."

"Don't remind me," I pouted.

Mark bent, pushing me back so he could take a nipple between his lips and suck it. He knows what pleases a girl, does Mark. His mouth was warm and wet and his tongue laved that brown nubbin until my hips started to squirm.

Then he went to the other breast.

"Mark, let's go into the bedroom," I pleaded.

"Leave the stockings on," he whispered as we came into the dimly lighted bedroom. My twin night table lamps have pink bulbs that cast a very romantic light over the pink tulle and the dark wood of my bed and furniture.

He let me go so he could feast his eyes on my bare back and shapely legs, not to mention my jellying buttocks, as I crossed the carpet to the bed and bent to turn down the covers. Mark is part voyeur, I think, which is all right with me because it is my bod that he likes to stare at in its various stages of dress and undress.

He came up behind me as I was bent over and fell to his knees. Next thing I knew his mouth was going up and down my bare thighs, above the nylons, right up to my buttocks, and then he was kissing them, hungrily and almost reverently.

"On the bed," he panted.

I felt like a love goddess, the way his eyes roved

my nakedness. Mark never hurried in his love-making, and when he said we must take our time, I knew I was in for a slow buildup to the moment of final spasm. Which was fine by me.

He came forward on his knees, he bent his head and then his mouth was sliding up my warm thighs to my hips and all over them, never coming too close to my pussylips, just skirting the red hairs of my pubes. In seconds, he had me whimpering and shuddering with absolute lust.

His hands gently parted my thighs, I knew he was staring between them and that he was seeing the moisture of my need. His mouth kissed up and down my inner thighs that he was holding open with his hands on my knees and pushing apart.

"Please, Mark. Please, darling," I breathed.

His head bent. I felt the brush of his lips across my genitals, the stroking of his tongue. I yelped, my hips lifted. I couldn't help it, the lustflames were alive in me; all my feelings and emotions were concentrated in just one spot.

My hands went to his head. I wanted to push him away, but couldn't, it felt too damn good, what he was doing to my private parts with his lips and tongue. My hips quivered and shook, I raised up to him, my fingers clawing at the bedspread.

"This is for saving my life," he would say. He was grateful and so was I.

It went on and on and I became a mindless thing

of flesh and pure animal instincts, awash in a sea of sexual pleasure. His tongue roved, it tickled, it teased and tormented—and then it satisfied. I wept and sobbed. I damn near fainted.

Only after a long time, a very long time, did Mark move from his kneeling position. He came up off the carpet and between my widespread thighs and then I felt his penis making a slow, slippery entrance between my futtering folds. He slid in slowly—only I knew what an effort of will it cost for him to be so easy about it all—and only when he had himself fully fleshed inside me, did he begin to move his hips.

I screamed. My legs came up and wrapped about him. I held onto him with both arms and we went off on a bed romp that carried up back and forth across the bed, to its very edge and then to the headboard as we bounced and rolled. How long it took, I'll never know. All I felt was that slide and withdrawal, that rigidity of male strength inside me and my own crazed reactions to its movements.

We finally brought up against the headboard, convulsing and shaking, and I clung to Mark Condon as if there were no tomorrow, hips beating my flesh at him, my breasts like rocks against his hairy chest.

At last we lay together, panting.

Mark kissed my throat, moved to draw away. I held him tighter, whispering, "No, don't move. Let's just fall asleep this way."

"I have to tell you about your orders, honey."

"It can wait. You can tell me in the taxi on the way to the airport. But let's sleep for a little while. Then if one of us wakes up, he can wake the other in some nice way and we can play some more."

Mark snuggled closer, arms about me. "You sure you'll be warm enough?"

"You can be my covers," I told him.

And he was, all during the night, one way or another.

Chapter Two

The British Overseas Airways Corporation jet-liner lifted off the ground with a purring of its big Rolls Royce engines. Below me, Mark Condon was standing on the walkway of the B.O.A.C. terminal, watching it rise upward toward the clouds. I couldn't see him, but I knew he was there. We'd had break-fast at the terminal before he walked me to the flight gate.

I felt pleasantly drowsy, settling back into my seat. Time enough to get out my sealed orders and read them. Right now I just wanted to unwind and let the cushions cradle me while the VC-10 swept me across half the world toward Hong Kong. I would have to go to work in Hong Kong. Right now I was still glowing from all that loving last night.

A stewardess tapped me, smiled into my opening eyes.

"Coffee?" she asked.

I shook my head. Coffee would keep me awake, and I needed sleep. Mark had been something more than demanding last night. If he wanted me to remember him while I was in Asia, he'd really set his brand on me. So I smiled and closed my eyes and drifted off to get that sleep I needed.

We ate lunch somewhere over Missouri on our flight path toward San Francisco. Over coffee and a cigarette, I slid my sealed orders out and opened the envelopes. The message was in code, but N.Y.M.P.H.O. agents have been trained to read its codes as a professor of English can scan a page of Dickens.

I would be met in Hong Kong, either at the airport or at the Peninsula Hotel where I had rooms, by an Englishman whose name was Derek Guyfford. I had no idea who he was or why he was to meet me, the message didn't say. But if Clinton Adams had arranged it, then it was important. I wondered how Guyfford would know me, or how I would know him.

The VC-10 let down in San Francisco for an hour stop-over to get its tanks refueled. I bought some reading material at the newsstand, then formed a line with the other passengers going to Hawaii.

We were going to stop overnight in Hawaii, the captain told us over the intercom, to give those passengers on their way to Hong Kong a change from being cooped up in their cabins. I thought that was a great idea, personally, it would give me a chance—I hoped—to take a dip in the ocean.

My stayover hotel in Hawaii was the Hilton Hawaiian Village, in the thirteen-story Village Tower from a window of which I could look out at some gorgeous gardens and cottages with thatched roofs. I shed my clothes, draped my body in a bikini and a beach cloak, and went out to take myself a dip in the ocean on Waikiki Beach. One thing about our N.Y.M.P.H.O. organization, they treat their operatives to the best.

I dined that night in the Golden Dragon Room, feasting my face on certain specialties of the house, which included a bowl of Won Ton soup, some egg foo yong, sweet and sour pork, and a dish of Cantonese fried chicken that almost melted in my mouth. There was a Mandarin salad, some oolong tea, and for dessert a big strawberry tart.

I was so stuffed when I moved away from the table, I could hardly walk. If I'd been wearing a girdle, it would have been killing me. I made it to my room, undressed and fell into bed.

Next morning the B.O.A.C. jet carried us westward over the Pacific. I had time to reflect on Derek Guyfford and what part he might play in my coming trackdown job. Of course, I had no idea of the men I was to search out and destroy, but I figured that in Red China or even in Hong Kong, for that matter, three Mafia triggermen ought to stand out pretty clearly. I didn't worry about them, I knew damn well a N.Y.M.P.H.O. man or woman would be meeting the incoming planes and photographing all the passengers. Surreptitiously, of course.

We came down in Tokyo and remained for an hour, then set off for Hong Kong. I dozed most of the way, I read all the printed material I had, and decided that I might have to do without sleep before I caught up with my Mafia buttons somewhere on the mainland.

Hong Kong is an island lying in the South China Sea, across from the Kowloon Peninsula. Its Victoria City is known as Hong Kong, too, but the nomenclature is wrong. It is a British Crown Colony, a mixture of smart new hotels and traditional old ones, a very thriving business district, a Chinese quarter, ladder streets and back alleys. You can get just about anything you want in Hong Kong, if you know the right palms to grease.

We droned down out of the clouds on a sunny afternoon, our VC-10 aimed at Kai Tak airport which is located across from Hong Kong on the peninsula. I studied the wide sweep of runways, the buildings and the waiting planes, and wondered what was going to happen to me before I climbed back onto a jet that would take me home. If I ever made it that far, that is.

The plane came down smoothly, the stewardess

warned us not to loosen our safety belts until the plane had come to a complete stop, and then I was gathering up my shoulder bag and lightweight coat and walking with the others toward the exit ramp.

I walked about twenty feet inside the terminal when a big blond man came bearing down on me, grinning from ear to ear in a sunbronzed face which made his light hair seem almost the color of flax. He wore a white suit and maroon shirt with a striped maroon-and-white tie.

His arms went around me, swept me off my feet.

"Hello, ducks," he breathed, and kissed me.

I said, when I could, "You'd better be Derek Guyfford."

"Right the first time, ducks. Have a good flight?"

I eyed his six feet four of muscular height—he looked like a civilized version of Tarzan, actually—and told myself this one could be a big help in a hand to hand fight. He was smiling with a little quirk to his lips as though he were enjoying a great joke at my expense. I was dying to hear what it was.

"The flight was fine. Maybe not as enthusiastic as the greeting, but it was pleasant enough," I said cautiously, still eyeing him suspiciously.

"Had to make it meaningful, pet. Can't tell who might be watching us. I've been spreading the word around that my bride to be is flying here from the colonies."

By colonies, he meant the United States. It's a

cute little way the British have of not recognizing the American Revolution and the War of 1812. He walked along with me, his hamlike hand holding my elbow protectively. He knew his way around, a mere wave of that huge hand made a taxi leap in our direction and the driver scurry off to get my bags.

Derek lighted up an Erik and surveyed me with half closed eyes through the smoke. The glint in his eyeballs told me he approved.

He said slowly, "Isn't going to be easy, what you're going to do."

"Why the bride-to-be bit?" I asked, disregarding his comment.

His blonde eyebrows rose. "We'll be together a lot, ducks. The Red Chinese frown on any sort of sex that isn't conducted between man and wife. At least they do, publicly. I thought it would be best if we pretended to be engaged."

It was my eyebrows that rose upward. "Sex? I'm not here for sex!"

His hand brushed that aside. "We'll be together a lot, you know. As my fiancee, things will be permitted that might not, if you were my secretary or female assistant."

The guy was damned attractive, my erogenous zones told me. But I wanted to put one thing straight between us. I was here to hunt down three Mafia buttons, not to bed down Derek Guyfford. I opened my mouth to tell him this when the taxi driver came hurrying back with my bags.

We got into the taxi, Derek assisting me. He practically pushed me in ahead of him so that my miniskirt rose upward and I felt sure his eyes were there along my nyloned legs and bare thighs, sizing up that part of me he hadn't seen before. As we settled in the seat, his eyes told me he approved of my understructure. I was glad of that, being a woman, but still and all.

"Now let's get one thing straight," I snapped.

"Of course, pet. Kim Chow is at the hotel in your room right now, waiting with the pictures."

"Kim Chow. Who's he? And—what pictures?"

He snubbed out what was left of the Erik in an ashtray. "Pictures of recent arrivals in Hong Kong, taken as they stepped off the plane. You're to select the men you feel are the killers you're hunting down."

"But I've never seen them before."

"Kim Chow will help you, there. He's a very knowledgeable man. He works for your organization, you know."

"I didn't, no. But—"

He smiled at me, grey eyes laughing. "Wait until you meet him. He heads a group of well-paid spies for sale to the highest bidder. Your group pays him well, and while he's on assignment for one organization, he's faithful to it. Which is quite a recommendation, these days in Hong Kong."

We went by way of Nathan Street to the Peninsula Hotel. Derek Guyfford had already registered me, so all I had to do was ask for the key to my room and up we went. As I walked in, a middle-aged Chinese man in that type of garment known as a Mandarin coat rose from a chair where he had been sitting and bowed to me.

"Kim Chow, I presume," I smiled, extending my hand.

He bowed over my hand, smiling in return, and then gestured at a leather attache case. "I have the pictures here, miss. If you will be so good as to look at them?"

I nodded, sat down and crossed my nyloned legs. Kim Chow handed me a number of glossy photographs. I ran through them casually at first, then more slowly.

I said, finally, "There were three of them. We feel they'll have flown from Kennedy or LaGuardia separately. Maybe they joined forces in Tokyo, where they felt they'd be safe. I'm not at all sure about this, it's just my hunch. At any rate, what I'm looking for is three men, Mafia types."

Kim Chow and Derek Guyfford exchanged glances. The Englishman nodded his blond head. I held out two pictures which showed three men walking side by side toward the terminal building.

"Those pictures were shot with a telescopic lens," Derek informed me. "And blown up by me in my laboratory after their development."

"You're a photographer?"

"It's why we're going into China," he nodded.

He took the pictures, studied them with Kim Chow looking over his shoulder. The snapshots showed a heavyset man who seemed about to burst out of his clothes, a smaller man with a moustache across his upper lip, and a lean, tall man with what appeared to be a scar running from the corner of his mouth to his chin. They were Latin types, dark, and with faces that seemed carved from wood, expressionless and hard.

Guyfford glanced at me. "You think these are the ones?"

I riffled through the other pictures. "They have to be. These others are tourists, or I miss my bet. Most of the other men are accompanied by women who appear to be their wives. These are the only three men who are together. Here and there," I lifted a snapshot to show him, "we have an individual who might be a member of the Mafia, but they're always alone, never with anyone else."

The Englishman nodded. "Makes sense to me."

Kim Chow smiled and bobbed his head. "It is what I have myself decided. I have developed a sort of sixth sense about such things, after many years at my work, Miss Delight, as you have yourself, I am sure, though your years do not compare with mine.

"And so I have taken it on my own to have these

three men shadowed by operatives in my employ. They all registered at the Imperial Hotel, which is just down the block from the Peninsula, on Nathan Road. They are being watched, night and day. So far there is nothing alarming to report."

I looked at Derek Guyfford. "Maybe I can catch up to them before they leave Hong Kong. It's certainly worth a try."

The Englishman looked amused. "If you think you can handle three at once, my hat's off to you."

I gave him my ingenue smile. "The night before I left New York I shot and killed two of their fellow Mafia members who tried to kill—execute, rather—a very good friend of mine. If you don't believe me, call the New York City police department and ask for Inspector Clinton Adams. He can fill you in on the details."

"I believe you," Guyfford said, though there was a doubt in his eyes.

Kim Chow began gathering up the pictures. He placed one in my hands, saying, "To be studied by you, so that you will know their faces."

"Give me a couple more, please. I want to check their way of walking, their mannerisms, if I can find any. A man can disguise his face, but very rarely his little habits."

Kim Chow beamed his approval. "You are a smart girl, Miss Delight. It is a pleasure to be working with you."

He left me about a dozen snapshots, taken of the three suspects as they moved toward the Kai Tak airport terminal building. I would study them after I'd had my hot shower, I told myself. Derek saw him to the door. When he came back, he stood a moment, staring down at me.

"I say, you're an odd one," he muttered after a time.

I looked from the pictures up at him. "How so, Derek?"

"You're beautiful, what you Americans call a sexpot. But you're smart. And, to judge by what you've told me, you're also pretty deadly with a gun."

"And karate, and judo, and Burmese boxing, and a knife. Oh yes, I've been well trained. It's why I draw such a salary that lets me live as I think my life should be lived."

He sat opposite me on a big blue hassock. "You know anything about photography?"

"Not the technical stuff. I can snap a picture and develop it, if that's what you mean. Part of my job."

Derek looked pleasantly surprised. 'That's great. You'll be my assistant as well as my fiancee, you understand. I've a visa to go into Red China and make photographs of life there. Of course, when we're taking the pictures the Red Chinese want us to take, we'll be very closely supervised. I intend doing a book on Red China, a pictorial work. It ought to make my fortune in the States, with things the way they are, China being so mysterious but opening up now to trade with the United States.

"You can carry a miniature camera, a Minox, one of those tiny things I ordered to be designed as a compact." He grinned wryly. "I was going to hire myself a girl photographer, anyhow, before I got the offer from N.Y.M.P.H.O. to work with them at a salary."

I laughed, "You'll have your cake and eat it, too."

"It's a lucky bit of business, I must admit. The way I figure it is this, you'll act the part of a dumb broad, just a sexy thing I take around with me to bed down. Now, now. I said you'd act the part, for the benefit of the Red Chinese who'll be watching us. I'll do all the picture snapping in public, you won't do a thing except hand me the cameras I'll need. So when we come to a part of their life that I'm sure they hide behind bamboo curtains, you'll get that compact out to powder your nose and snap a picture or two."

"Where's the compact? I'll have to study it, get used to it, you know. Maybe I even ought to take a picture or two while we're in Hong Kong, to get the feel of the thing."

Derek Guyfford beamed. "An excellent idea. I'll go get it, you can relax for a few hours, and tonight we'll have dinner together, maybe you'll even get that chance to practise your picture taking."

"I'd like that," I said truthfully.

"If you're keen on Indian food, we could try the Bombay Oriental. Or if you prefer something different, say a meal on the water at the harbor, we could go to the Tai Pak or the Sea Palace."

My eyes lighted up at that idea. "I've heard of these floating restaurants, but I've never seen them."

"Then it's the water for us."

When he was gone I stripped down and walked naked from the bedroom adjoining my little living room into the shower. I soaped my breasts, my crotch, my sleek pink skin very carefully. I would be wearing a creation by Paco Rabanne tonight—if I were going into Red China with Derek Guyfford, there wouldn't be much chance to wear evening gowns, I figured—and so I wanted to appear as glamorous as possible. After I'd dried off and dusted some powder on myself, I turned back the bed covers and flopped into bed.

I fell asleep at once and didn't even dream.

It was nearing dusk when I awoke, completely refreshed. I dabbed some Chanel perfume where it might do the most good, wrapped a pair of filmy bikini panties about my hips, and slithered my bouncing curves inside the Paco Rabanne outfit. This consisted of blue velvet slacks and a top that was nothing more than a number of tinted discs strung together quite artfully, under which was my naked body. My feet went into blue evening pumps. The mirror told me I looked absolutely eatable.

So did Derek Guyfford's face when he saw me. His eyes got big, his mouth fell open and he gave me the happiest grin I'd seen in ages.

"I'm not too—exposed—for Hong Kong, am I?" I wondered.

"You'll make eyes pop, love."

Derek would make a few eyes pop, himself. He wore a summer formal, with cummerbund, and his lean height and craggy good looks, with that blond mane on top of his head, would make feminine hearts pound with erotic eagerness. My own did a bump and grind too, as his grey eyes stared down into mine.

We took a taxi to the waterfront and there Derek hired a water taxi to ferry us through a glittering paradise of high-sterned junks and pirogues, all fitted with colored paper lanterns behind which flickered the lights of innumerable candles. It was a fairy world with the dark blue waters reflecting back those lights so that it seemed we floated between worlds as the silent woman worked her oar to carry us slowly and almost silently, with only a rippling of water at prow and stern to tell where we went, toward a big houseboat-like restaurant with paper lanterns adding to its exotic setting.

The harbor was quiet, cool, with a faint breeze coming from the peninsula. The moon was a big silver ball overhead and for a while I was able to forget I was working for N.Y.M.P.H.O. and here in Hong

Kong to kill three men.

The pirogue bumped the Sea Palace. An attendant came running to catch a rope and hold the boat steady as Derek got out and bent to assist me. My eyes touched what looked like a totem pole. It was, I was informed by the attendant, a spirit-pole placed there to frighten away evil spirits so we might enjoy our meal in peace.

The restaurant was of wood; it shone like gold in the moonlight, Derek told me as he guided me across the deck toward a doorway, and from its deck, during the daytime, you could shop for silks and velvets, for saris from India and lovely cheongsams from the mainland, for a thousand and one things.

We were seated at a window overlooking the harbor. We could see the mountains in the background. the harbor lights that flickered and danced, moving junks with their batwing sails framed against the moon. A little paper lantern hung from a silver holder on the table. Derek lifted the menu, began to make suggestions.

"To begin with, rice wine, especially flavored as only the Sea Palace can do it," said Derek, at which the waiter who apparently knew him well, bowed and confirmed the compliment.

And while we sipped the rice wine, which was very tasty indeed, and maybe strong as well, because I got a warm glow on, Derek set about ordering the meal.

"A little of many things," he told me with a smile. "This is the way to eat an Oriental meal. For instance, we shall begin with the curried shrimp, a true delicacy, but we must not eat too much of it. For there will come the rice pilau, the shredded Bombay duck, and finally the curried lamb. I do hope you like curry?"

We did not hurry, I was not anxious to go back to my hotel room to sleep alone. I was refreshed by my nap, and Derek's constant interest in my disced jacket under which he could see my naked breasts and even my nipples when a disc or two slipped out of place, told me he wasn't the least bit bored.

There was hot green tea afterward, to wash everything down. We smoked cigarettes and talked about little, inconsequential matters, nothing about my job and his, there might be ears to overhear what we said. I think the entire meal took three hours.

When we were ready to leave, the Englishman said, "A pirogue ride around the harbor, Cherry. How about it?"

"Love to," I murmured.

The floating restaurants pay the fares of the water taxis which bring them customers, so Derek hired the woman and her boat to ride us around under the big moon, in order that I might take in the night sights of Victoria Harbor. It was very peaceful. It was hard to believe there were three killers in this city ready to flee into mainland China and establish criminal links with the tongs that operated so secretly there. And that it was my job to stop and kill them.

I let my mind and eyes drift as the pirogue drifted, seemingly without a goal. I trailed my fingers in the water, I saw the water shops, shuttered now in the night time. I saw small pirogues with hooped coverings over them, where dim lights burned and occasionally a girl laughed or a man murmured passionately. These were the floating brothels, Derek informed me when I questioned him. Bangkok had them, so did Hong Kong and all the international cities along the Asiatic eastern coastline.

Derek put his arm about me after a time, it was to be expected. I snuggled up to him, let my head rest on his shoulder. After all, it was part of my job, I suppose, to keep him happy. He was my cover in Red China, he knew the language as well as Mao Tse-tung, and the ways of the people who lived on the mainland. Besides, I liked him.

He did not offer to kiss me, which was a surprise.

Oh, he wanted to; as a woman I could tell that, but I think he felt I'd be insulted or some such nonsense. Anyhow, he contented himself with hugging me from time to time while he discoursed on Hong Kong, explaining that its original name was Victoria after the queen, and that it was made up of two major cities, Victoria and Kowloon. It had been ceded to the English in 1841. It was just an island where two thousand fishermen lived, at that time. Well over two million people lived there now, to say nothing of the Chinese who make their way from the mainland to freedom from their Red masters.

As we neared the waterfront docks at the foot of Connaught Street where we'd taken the water taxi, I saw a lantern moving back and forth. I sat up, peered through the mists gathering on the harbor waters.

"You think that's for us, that lantern?"

Derek stared a moment, counted the irregular swingings of that light under his breath, sat up and cursed. "It's Kim Chow," he muttered at last. "I've worked with him before, ducks, that's one of his ways of signalling me when something's come up I ought to know. As for now, for instance."

He said something to the woman in a low voice and she hurried the sweeps of her oar so that the pirogue slid more swiftly through the oily waters of Victoria Harbor. He and I were both leaning forward on the edge of the thwart, we could make out Kim Chow after a time, even through the mists.

He was peculiarly agitated, and he paced up and down as the lantern swung in his hand. When he saw that he had our attention, he blew out the candle and stood in the dimness of moonlight with the mists about him, waiting patiently.

Derek paid the woman with a large banknote. She bobbed her head and gave us a toothy grin as we stepped onto the dock. I guess she'd made a month's wages in a single night because she called out for us to take her boat next time.

Then Kim Chow was leading us away from the wharf toward a waiting car. He said, "Our birds have flown, Guyfford. Two of them by plane after having purchased tickets to Chungking on a U.T.A. jetliner, the other went into the Chinese quarter."

Derek looked at me. I said, "This one that went into the Chinese quarter. Maybe I ought to go after him."

Kim Chow said, "He went into a very bad section, Miss Delight. Hopheads and prostitutes, men fleeing from British law, runaway sailors, all hole up there. It is dangerous at any time, most especially after dark."

Kim Chow said, "I will loan you one of my cars. If you insist on going, that is. I must repeat, you may never come out of there alive." His eyes touched me, ran over my expensive clothes. "In those garments, everyone in that quarter will know you for a thrill seeker, you will be like a chicken in a den of foxes."

I said grimly, "I'm one chicken who can fight back. I'm going."

After all, I drew a damn good paycheck from N.Y.M.P.H.O. for risking my neck in places such as those, where our quarry is sometimes known to go. I needed a gun, however, and my service revolver was back in my hotel room.

Kim Chow smiled, reached into his pocket and produced a pearl-handled Savage. "A thirty-two calibre gun, Miss Delight. Very accurate, without too much of a kick. It will be my pleasure to loan it to you for the night's work. That way, no one can possibly trace the bullet to you, if you should succeed."

I tucked the Savage into my handbag, looked at Derek. "You don't have to come, Derek. This is my job, not yours."

"What do you take me for?" he asked grumpily. "Kim, you got another gun on you?"

The Hong Kong man chuckled, lifted out a Webley. "This will suit you, Derek, it also is accurate and without too much of a kick."

"How many of those things do you carry on you?" I wondered.

He laughed softly. "I have two more, in case I myself run into trouble. Each gun is fully loaded as are my own. Oh, and one more thing. I have operatives with walkie-talkies in the Chinese quarter. We will speak to them before you go in there, if you will be so good."

We were at the little Austin car. Kim Chow got in, fiddled with his two-way radio set. He called into the microphone, "Lem Duck, Kim Chow here. Have you followed our man?"

"I have," came a metallic voice. "He has gone into the Blue Goose."

Kim Chow sighed, glancing at us. "The Blue Goose is a combination brothel and gambling den, opium den and general all around vice parlor."

"Sounds like fun."

Kim Chow glowered. "You must not be so light-hearted, Miss Delight. It is a bad, bad place you are going into. You must be very careful." He smiled faintly. "I do not warn Derek Guyfford, you see. He knows whereof I speak."

Derek nodded, putting a hand on the Webley butt. "I'll learn tonight how good you are with a gun, Cherry. Or as a judo expert, too, in all probability. All right, let's get cracking."

Kim Chow got out of the car, we got in, Derek sliding behind the wheel, since he knew the city. I leaned across Derek, asked, "Kim Chow, which one of the three is it, who went into the Chinese quarter?"

"The small man, the one with the moustache."

My hand tightened around the butt of the Savage in my handbag. I put my eyes to the front, staring at Connaught Road as we moved along it, then sat back as Derek drove along the still-crowded streets toward the Chinese section.

"We'll have to leave the car, you know," Derek said after a time. "There are so-called 'ladder streets' in the Chinese section which are really flights of steps up and down the slopes."

"Okay by me. You know where the Blue Goose is?"

"I know," he said. Rather grimly, I thought.

Then he was parking and we got out of the car. I studied a ladder street to my right, that seemed to go up into emptiness. There were small, mean little houses on all sides, this was the outlying part of the Chinese quarter. I took a firmer grip on my handbag that held the pearl-handled Savage and turned to smile at Derek.

He nodded at me reassuringly, caught my elbow and led me toward the steps. Up we went, with the cool air filled with the smells of chicken and rice, together with other odors not so pleasant. It was not a nice place to be, it sent the shivers down my back and I wouldn't have been surprised to see half a dozen tong hatchetmen spring out of the shadows at us.

But we made our way uneventfully up the steps and along a narrow cobblestoned street where little shop signs hung like banners from small poles. The stores were shuttered, closed and dark at this time of night, and our footsteps echoed hollowly as we walked along.

Here and there we made out dim figures in doorways, and once I saw two young men pause in their walking to turn and look at us. Maybe Derek's size and obvious strength scared them off, or maybe they went for reinforcements, because they turned suddenly and hastened away.

Derek's fingers tightened on my arm. Up ahead was a sign in the shape of a goose, lighted blue with neons. It was our destination.

"Take a deep breath," Derek said softly. "It may be the last clean air you'll ever breathe."

I did what he said, and my knees began to shake.

Chapter Three

The door opened for us into a blue dimness where a pretty girl naked to her navel, bowed and smiled a greeting. She was the doorlady, I guessed, because after she had intoned her greeting, she went back and sat on the leather-topped stool that was her roosting place.

A waiter, a male this time, bowed to us, brought us through a hallway lighted only by a very faint electric bulb behind a blue lampshade, into a large room panelled in wood and hung with decorated art forms. Tables were set in the shadows, a number of men and women were eating and drinking quietly.

"You want eat, drink?" asked the waiter.

Derek handed him a pound note. "Something more lively, Tom. The show, the whole works. I want the lady to be impressed."

The impassive oriental eyes touched me, fell

away. Tom nodded, led a path between the tables to a wooden door. This he swung open and now I could catch the acrid scent of opium smoke. It was very faint, only a mere hint, and Derek whispered that there was an opium den in the cellar.

"I can arrange a tour, if you'd like," he said quietly.

I nodded. After all, opium dens were something I'd only read about in Fu Manchu novels or the like. I would dearly love to see the real thing. Besides, my quarry might be down there, sucking at a pipe.

The waiter listened as Derek whispered and passed him another pound note. He brought us into a large room that was almost black in darkness. The only light was a flood, beamed down on a small stage. You heard the clink of glasses, the breathing of people all around you, the soft scurry of feet as waiters filled glasses and brought such food as might be desired. Nobody paid us any heed. Every eye was on the stage.

You could scarcely help looking.

A naked girl was on a bed, the bed was so low the on-lookers were almost on eye-level with its top, and the girl had her pale thighs spread wide apart and was fingering her hairless slit. I gulped, eyes glued to those wet, moving fingers, the rising and falling hips.

"This way," Derek whispered and I turned obediently to the right and followed him and the waiter past some tables and to another door which opened onto a flight of wooden steps.

The steps went downward into a cellar which was faintly lighted. There was bluish smoke here, and the smell of the opium was very strong. I blinked as it ate at my eyeballs, and brushed away the pain. I had to have my eyes at their full twenty-twenty vision, if I were to pick out my Mafia quarry.

The waiter bowed, accepted another note, whispered that he would be waiting for us at the top of the stairs when we were done. I guess he figured we wanted to smoke a pipe, maybe, but Derek put me straight.

"Tom knows I don't go in for it, he knows we're just here to get a cheap thrill. He thinks he knows that you are my bedmate for the evening and that I'm hoping, what with a sniff of these opium fumes—opium's supposed to be an aprodisiac, you know, but it isn't—and looking at the exhibition going on upstairs, it will get you in the mood."

He chuckled, added, "I hope it does, but that isn't why we're here."

We went side by side between the bunks where Chinese and Europeans lay, long clay pipes between their lips at which they puffed drowsily. There were some who were deep in those dreams the poppy brings, sprawled almost lifelessly on the thin mattresses, their cares forgotten. At each bunk-bed was a small table where a lamp, a packet of matches and the other paraphernalia needed to light up an opium pipe was placed by the old man with the long white beard sitting in a corner, who was the sole attendant.

We walked the rows of bunks, we glanced into every face.

Moustache-man was not here.

At the foot of the staircase, I glanced at Derek, shrugging. "He's probably upstairs in the exhibition room," I said softly.

"Not unlikely," Derek nodded. "I doubt he'd go for opium. Your marijuana, perhaps, or even heroin, but scarcely opium. Still, you can never tell, and it was well worth our while to have a look."

"Upstairs, then," I nodded.

Derek chuckled, "I figured him for more of a sex nut, anyhow."

The waiter opened the door at our knock and brought us to a table near a wall which afforded a good view of the entire room. We sat, he pushed the table closer, nodded when Derek ordered champagne, and disappeared.

My eyes ran around the room. There were men here, some with women, some by themselves or in the company of another man. It took me perhaps five minutes to locate Moustache-man, seated at a table close to the brilliantly lighted steps. He was hunched forward, eyes fastened on the naked girl who was in the throes of an orgasm.

My stare touched the girl, clung.

Her fingers were buried in the gaping red gash between her quivering thighs. Love liquid ran from her over her fingers, onto her thighs. Her hips rose and fell, she squealed and yelled, and her breasts shook like jelly in a windstorm. It was an exciting spectacle, no wonder my quarry couldn't tear his eyes away.

The girl went on and on, fingers moving like pistons in a sheathing, wet and glistening in the light. Her legs lifted her up and off the little bed so she touched it only with her heels and head. When she took her wet hands away, which she did from time to time to let the onlookers see her private parts, I could make out the quivering length of her enlarged clitoris. It must have been four inches long. She was a freak, in a way, I guess. It was a way that pleased the man with the moustache, because he couldn't take his eyes off her.

"He'll probably hire her for an upstairs room," whispered the Englishman.

"There are upstairs rooms?"

"You're an innocence, ducks. Of course there are. Why do you think the girls like that put on such acts? To excite the customers. Then when they get hot enough, the waiter reminds them that they can have the privacy of a bedroom with one of the performers."

"Some of the men have women here," I pointed out.

"What makes you think the women don't go for a bit of uncluttered sex, pet? Some women have lesbian tendencies, you know. They lead boring, humdrum lives. A place like this is right up their alley. They come with their husbands who get to lay a strange girl, maybe the husband even gets excited by the way his wife and the girl put on a lesbian show for him."

My inner thighs were crawling with heat. I could understand how a man felt, watching the performer as she toyed with that immense clitoris. She was working herself into another fit of vulvolimia. And she wasn't the only one getting excited.

The waiter brought the champagne.

The cork popped, he poured the bubbley. Derek and I lifted our glasses, drank. While this was going on, the naked girl was reaching for an electric vibrator, raising it to show to the eyes that were fastened on her, then held the lips of her pussy open and inserted it.

When she switched on the current, all hell broke loose.

She screamed with that vibrating dildo working away inside her love channel. Her buttocks beat the bed, she tossed her head from side to side, she wept and moaned. It was an exhibition to warm the cockles of a man's heart. And something more than his cockles, too.

I squirmed in my chair, muttering. "Nobody can

walk out on something like that," I breathed. "These men have to get relief."

"And well the management of the Blue Goose knows it, love. That's where they make their money, you know. Each room and a performer to go with it costs fifty pounds. Roughly, two hundred and fifty American dollars. Figure fifty small rooms on the upstairs floors, night after night, and you can guess at the profits."

My eyes slid sideways at him. "Do you have fifty pounds on you, Derek?"

He grinned as his eyes met mine. He nodded curtly. I said lightly, "We'll have to take a room, you know. The moustache will, and that will be the best place to kill him, up there in a little room."

"You're a bloodthirsty wench."

My face hardened. "He killed Bill Tomkins, he and those other two hired guns. It's my job to eliminate him. And—them."

"I know, I know," he said hastily, not wanting to spoil my mood.

"We'll wait, of course, until he leaves."

"Of course," Derek said wryly.

My hand slid to his lap. He was big down there, long and hard as a steel bar. "My, my," I whispered, fingers tightening around him.

"Better let go, ducks," he muttered hoarsely.

My fingers let go. At the same time, the exhausted girl crawled off the low bed and staggered toward the curtains at one side of the stage. She was scarcely out of view when a girl and a young man came running in from the other side of the stage, both of them wearing only cloaks.

I saw my Mafia suspect beckon a waiter.

The man and the girl came to a stop on either side of the bed, facing the audience. They let their black, dragon-ornamented cloaks slip down. Each was stark naked, and the man had a semi-erection. They turned and walked about, the girl smiling genially at everyone in the audience, her eyes diamond-bright where the floodlights caught the eyeballs. I thought she must be high on hashish.

They turned and ran toward each other, meeting with a slap of flesh and kissing hungrily. The girl worked her naked body against that of the youth, rubbing her big breasts to his shaven chest, letting her red-nailed fingers slide up and down his body.

A waiter detached himself from the little group assembled in a corner of the room and began his walk toward the table where my quarry sat, staring at the couple just above his head. I tried to watch them, but my stare was drawn to the couple who were now drawing away from each other so the man could run his hands over the bulging breasts with the huge red nipples and the girl could take his protruding manhood between her fingers and caress it slowly.

She slipped to her knees before him, held his

elongated penis and began drawing her tongue up and down its quivering length, very slowly. The floodlamps caught the glisten of her saliva on that bulging shaft, added to the erotic interest of the onlookers. She cupped her breasts, captured his swollen spear, began working her breastflesh on it.

The young man quivered and jerked to that pleasure.

Below him, the man with the moustache was speaking to the waiter in low tones. I saw a banknote change hands. The waiter walked away.

Now the girl was opening her mouth, poising it above the purplish penishead jutting upward from between her breasts. The audience was very still, scarcely moving. Only the youth's indrawn breath could be heard, and the slurpingly moist sound of the girl closing her lips over what she held prisoner and lifting her head, letting it fall.

I know I was reacting to the sight. My breasts were like pale white rocks, my nipples hurt, they were so stiff. Beside me, Derek Guyfford was leaning forward to cover his own male excitement. Between my legs, a telltale moisture was commencing.

The girl did not bring the young man to orgasm, she was gentle, delicate in her oral ministrations. He cried out harshly from time to time, and this might have been a signal between them, for after a time she stopped and he helped her to her feet. With both hands she caught his rod and moved it back and forth across her belly.

The youth turned her so the audience could see her pale buttocks, then guided her toward the bed.

She knelt on the narrow end, her backside facing the eyes staring at the stage. Slowly she inched her knees apart so the onlookers would be able to stare between her thighs.

She was wildly excited. Her genitals were wet, the red labia covered with a greyish foam, thrusting out like the lips of a hungry mouth. And her clitoris, while not so large as that of the other girl, was big enough to be perfectly visible.

Standing to one side of her, her partner began to tease that scarlet sex-mouth. He used his fingers, touching the enlarged clitoris, moving it about. The girl wailed, her hips bucked. They did not hurry, they were here to get the customers so hot they'd all be hiring assignation rooms at fifty pounds per each. The girl began to mewl in the grip of her intense lust, after a few seconds.

"Please! Oh my God! Please put it in! Please. . . ."

The male refused those beggings, he went on tease-torturing her.

Out of the corner of my eye I caught sight of the waiter approaching the table where moustache-man was sitting. He had to tap the Mafia boy on the shoulder half a dozen times before he could rouse him from that tail trance induced by the sight of the performers.

He took a key from the waiter. More money changed hands. I strained my eyes trying to read the room number on the disc attached to the key, but could not. My elbow nudged Derek.

"He's bought himself a room, better get one for us before they run out."

Derek was as much in a state of copulation coma as was the Mafia button. His eyes were glazed, his breath was coming fast and shallow. But the haze of desire fled from his eyes, he lifted an arm and wriggled a finger.

The waiter came toward us, impassive.

"A room, please," the Englishman said.

"Fifty pounds."

Derek handed over the money, we waited.

I hoped moustache-man would also wait a little before heading upstairs. I wanted to see the end of the act. Maybe he did too, because he sat hunched over his table, occasionally remembering to drink from his nearly empty glass. I supposed his mouth was very dry.

The man on the stage got up onto the bed, now, right behind the yawning thighs of his love partner. The audience could see his testicles hanging between his own thighs and the inordinate length of his phallus. He took that shaft in a hand, guided it. We could see it nuzzle at the scarlet lips which seemed to open for it, then disappear inside.

And now the bed began to move, very slowly.

It was on some kind of turntable, of course. And it moved to let the audience watch what was happening from every angle. We got a side view, with the youth drawing his organ out of the clutching vaginal tunnel that held it; he posed that way for several seconds, then drove it deep again.

Derek began making funny noises.

"Pet, I can't take any more of this. It's too much for a fellow to endure, you know."

"We can't go until he does. Be patient."

Now the youth was reaching under the girl and grabbing her breasts, shaking them wildly, as one might balloons filled with water. The nipples danced erratically and the girl herself was twisting, sobbing, banging her behind back into the youth's belly, working herself on the phallatic piston driving smoothly in and out of her.

They came to a crashing finale, convulsed, the man clinging to the female under him, his weight slowly driving her toward the bed. They lay there, still moving, savoring the aftermath of their lust.

"Let's go," I breathed.

Derek Guyfford glanced at me in surprise, then turned his head to stare at my quarry. "But he's still here."

"He just grabbed up the key that waiter gave him. He'll be along in a second or two. By leaving ahead of him, he won't think we're following him."

I was reasonably certain that no such thought was

in his head, all he could think about was the little Chinese doll with the over-developed clitoris. Still, I was on a job for N.Y.M.P.H.O., and I was taking no chances.

We moved toward a side door. Derek had his arm about my waist and was stroking my hip with his right hand as we walked. If he was feeling the way I was, my only wonder was that he didn't throw me down over a table and have his jollies with me. But I've heard the English are very staid people.

His hand slid downward as we went through the curtained doorway, it moved lazily over my wobbling buttocks, damn near naked except for the bikini panties. Save for those panties and the Paco Rabanne blue velvet slacks and the disced jacket, plus my blue evening pumps, I was naked.

I pretended to glance up at him, but my eyes went to the table where my quarry had been sitting. He was on his feet, moving awkwardly—because of his erection, I supposed—toward the same doorway through which we were passing.

A narrow flight of worn wooden steps were before us. We went up them, yours truly first so Derek could reach under the blue discs of my evening gown jacket and touch my breasts. He had a light touch, my erogenous zones clamored for more of the same. It took a distinct effort of will not to turn around and give myself to him, right on the stairs. I reminded myself I was working, I was here to kill a man, and the job came first.

"What do we do first?" he croaked as we came to the upstairs floor.

"We go into our room. What number is it?"

"Six," he muttered, glancing down at the key-disc.

"We were right after the guy with the moustache," I murmured, leading the way down the uncarpeted hall. "Let's hope he has five."

I opened a door, went into a room furnished with a bed and a washstand, a straightbacked chair and a clothesrack. I had time for one glance, then Derek was shoving himself against me, his steel-hard erection nudging my blue-velvet-covered buttocks, his hands under my breasts and shaking them.

"Wait, Derek—wait," I panted.

"You want it, ducks. You know you do."

"Who wouldn't, after seeing what they were doing on that stage? But fun comes last. I have a job to do."

"We've got to get the hell out of here fast, once you do that. You don't think we'll have time for hanky panky then, do you?"

My moist vulva told me he was making sense. I mean, after all, there was no hurry about this. Moustache-man was going to screw the girl he'd hired, he'd take his time about it (I hoped), which would give us the time to do something about that rigid penis making black and blue marks all over my buttocks.

So I turned, I thew my arms about him and gave the Englishman my open mouth and tongue. Now his shaft was playing games with my mons veneris and from time to time its swollen head nudged my standing clitoral bud. My hips worked into his, I savored this enjoyment With a blood-pounding delight that damn near made me swoon.

I heard a door open and close, even through the slamming of my pulses. I drew back. Somebody had come into the room next door.

I stepped back from Derek, put my hands to my blue-disced evening apparel jacket, and lifted it off. My breasts came out into the open, bouncing. Derek stared at them with glazed eyes, tongue rimming his lips.

"You like titty?" I whispered.

"Oh, ducks—do I!"

His mouth swooped, wrapped lips about a nipple. He sucked hungrily, fiercely, so that it almost hurt. But it was a good hurt, I let my eyelids fall and leaned forward, pushing more of my right breast into his mouth.

Maybe the pleasure of his nipple-sucking made my hearing more sensitive, because I heard footsteps moving about in the room beside ours, and a door opening again. Then I heard muted voices.

"Took your time about it," a man said.

"I had to shower, mista. You want me nice and clean, don't you?"

"I want you, that's all."

"Lemme take my dress off."

I tried to hear what else they said, but their speech degenerated into moans and gasps, even as our own. Derek was moving from one nipple to the other, and I took advantage of his thelerthic trance to work at his clothes. I wanted him buck naked. It was a little difficult, with his lips working away on my teats, but I managed it, getting his summer formal jacket off and then his shirt and undoing his belt and running down his fly.

My hand went into that fly just as his pants started slipping. My fingers wrapped around it. I was in the mood for loving, my memory cells had forgotten all about Mark Condon.

He put his hands to my slacks, shoved them and my bikini panties down. I did the same with his shorts. Now we were both naked, with him standing in his pooled trousers, me in my blue velvet evening slacks draped about my ankles. Our nude bodies came together and we moved lazily, kissing.

The girl next door cried out.

I think Derek heard it too, because the clutch of his arms about my naked body got even tighter, mashing my breasts. I squirmed to the touch of his palms on my quivering buttocks. Then those fingers tightened in my assflesh and lifted.

I went up into the air, my legs parting.

Derek's erection slid between my widened thighs.

My hand went down to catch and guide it. There was very little foreplay, we were both too excited by the sex exhibition we'd been watching. I felt him glide up between my labia, sliding into my genital tunnel.

I sank down and more and more of his shaft went up inside me. I was in a nookie nirvana, my senses swirled around me in a whirlpool of erotic excitement. I sobbed as my hips lifted and fell, rose and drove. I circled them, I beat them at him. My legs were twined about his legs, he held me with his hands fastened in my behind.

"Walk," I whimpered. "Walk around."

He took a step, his male spear sliding sideways inside me. I mewled, my legs tightened, Derek Guyfford was big and strong, I felt he could carry my hundred and ten pounds around without too much trouble. How right I was! He took slow strides, savoring each frictional rub of our exacerbated genitals. I crooned, I sobbed, I lurched and rammed my hips on what they held.

His striding brought us to the wall of the room next door.

As if to give himself a little rest, Derek let me lean my bare back against cool wood. We began to work away in what the Arabs call *el keurchi*, which means 'belly to belly', lifting and falling as relentlessly as the sea.

There was only one thing wrong.

I kept going backwards.

Then it dawned on me. My spine was against the cool wood of a door that was opening into the room next door. In our excitement I'd forgotten all about it. A careless chambermaid, if they had such things at the Blue Goose, must have forgotten to close and lock it.

My hand slapped Derek lightly on the shoulder. He opened his eyes. My head turned and I found we were a step or two inside the room adjacent to our own, and that my quarry was stark naked on the bed, a dreamy smile on his lips and the same naked girl who'd been performing solo on the stage bed was crouched above his body, her mouth filled with his male organ. Her head was rising and falling slowly.

Derek took a step backward, then another.

I reached down, brought the door with us. I left a little crack so I could peep through. Meanwhile, Derek was still performing with genital gusto, his shaft driving in and out of me, drowning me in diddling delight. My own hips surged to meet his own, we were in a voyeuristic heaven.

Because we were both watching through that little crack between door and jamb, we saw the girl with her naked body kneeling between his hairy thighs, her brown hair falling loosely, we saw the lift and drop of her head. The man on the bed was groaning, his hips rising, falling.

The girl was too smart to let him spend too soon. She had to earn her money, she didn't want the man complaining. She rose up away from him, paused to lick her lips and stare down at her lollypop. It quivered, wet and long, before her stare.

"Hey," protested the man.

"Want to play with me now," said the girl.

I figured there was little or no chance of his noticing the partially open door. He had eyes only for her bowl-shaped breasts that dangled and swung as she started her crawl over him. The girl paused to let one breast swing and bump against his erection, using that breast to caress him. I could hear the hiss of his inhaled breath at the touch.

Then she was crouched above his chest, her thighs splayed wide apart, and Moustache-man was gluing his eyeballs to that red, wet gash spread so enchantingly for his stare. She hunkered down, squatting frog-fashion, right over his face. He could see nothing but those genitals she was showing him.

It would have been easy to kill him.

All I would have to do was stand here and fire the Savage .32 which Kim Chow had given me. The only trouble with that was, the girl would hear the sound and see us, and be almost deafened by the noise of the shot, which would reverberate from wall to wall of the whole damn building.

There had to be a better way.

I left the door open just a crack as Derek began

backing up toward the bed. I wanted on that bed just as badly as he did, but I was afraid that my quarry would give us the slip. I freely admit I wasn't reasoning too clearly at that moment, Derek was pounding away and I was pounding right back at him, I said the hell with it and let him push me down on the covers.

We went at it hot and heavy.

We rolled and bounced across that bed and back and forth for I don't know how long, and we enjoyed every minute of it. I peaked again and again, and I know he did too, at least twice. He was pretty great with the staying powers, was the Englishman.

All good things must come to an end, and pretty soon I found myself cramped in a ball under him, with him sobbing out his delirium in my ear as his body wept its own special brand of love tears inside me.

We clung together, shivering.

Then I whispered, "Let me hit the john, honey."

He drew back. I heard what seemed to be an echo of my own voice from the room next door. The girl was saying, "No more, not now. I gotta go take care of myself. I'll be back."

"I want the whole night, Su Fo. I gotta job to do that's going to keep me corked up like a bottle in the ocean, I got to get my rocks off in one night."

Su Fo giggled. I heard the pad of bare feet, the slither of a dress. Probably there was a house rule about the girls running around the corridors bareass. I lay beside Derek and tried to get my strength back.

Su Fo said, "You take little nap. I be back."

"You'd better be. I paid double for the use of this room all night long, and I'm not going to waste a penny of it."

Again she giggled. I heard the door open and close.

My hands pushed Derek back and away. I slid noiselessly across the bed as he watched me dreamily. I put a forefinger to my lips to caution him to silence, and jerked my head at the slightly open door into the next room.

Derek sat up, alarmed. He mouthed the words, "You can't just walk in on them. They'll bring the house down around us."

I whispered back, "Leave this to me."

My handbag was within easy reach. I lifted and opened it, drew out the Savage revolver. Then I swung about and walked toward the door.

Chapter Four

I tiptoed to the door, peeped through the crack.

My quarry lay naked on his front in the bed. He was probably following the advice of the sing-song girl and grabbing forty winks. I didn't know whether he was asleep or not, but I was stark naked and my bare feet would make no sound when I went into his room. My eyes went around the room slowly.

There was a pillow on the floor near the foot of the bed. Maybe he'd used it under Su Fo when he'd been banging her, I didn't know, but it seemed likely enough. When he wanted to take his snooze, he'd merely kicked it off the bed. He lay with his head pillowed on his bare arms in lieu of a pillow.

I stepped silently into the room.

Gun in hand, I crossed the room. My quarry may have been exhausted, I felt sure his guard was down. Who would want to kill him in Hong Kong? At any rate, he was breathing steadily, without a break. Once I even thought I heard him snore, but that was merely wishful thinking.

I bent, lifted the pillow. I folded it around the Savage.

My feet made no sound as I came to the edge of the bed. I bent forward, the pillow hiding the gun. I let my hand bring the gun almost within touching distance of the back of his head. He slept on.

Under my breath I murmured, "This is for Bill Tomkins!"

I squeezed the trigger and blew half his head off.

The sound was like a thunderclap in my ears. I took one glance at the red ruin of his skull and ran for the open door. I closed it, stood leaning against it.

Derek was on the edge of the bed, staring at me with wide eyes. "I heard it," he said, "but it wasn't as bad as I thought it would be."

"I used a pillow. Come on, get dressed. We've got to get out of here." I ran for my blue velvet slacks, the disced jacket. In seconds, I was ready and Derek, moving faster than I thought he could, was almost fully dressed. We didn't wait for him to put on his tie, we just beat feet into the hall and toward the stairs.

As we started down the treads, I risked one glance behind me. Su Fo was coming along the corridor on her way to her client. In a few seconds, her screams would be slamming from cellar to roof.

"Hurry!" I yelped at Derek.

We were through the restaurant and moving along the narrow corridor toward the front door when we heard her scream. My nerves jangled and I came damn close to echoing that yell, but the door-lady seemed unconcerned. She didn't even look up at the ceiling.

Then it came to me.

The sing-song girls encounter a lot of sadists from the audience, men who want to humiliate them, cause them pain. Usually such men paid extra for these divertissements, maybe the girl even got some of that extra bread. And when they were hurt too badly, some of them screamed.

The door opened. I plunged through to step out on the cobblestones. Derek was beside me in a moment. Then we really ran for about a hundred yards, until we figured we were safe from pursuit.

"There may not even be any chase," the Englishman told me.

I stared at him. "Nobody to come after us?"

"Not even to ask any questions," he chuckled. "Here in the Chinese quarter, men or women get killed almost every night. The authorities rarely interfere, unless one of their own, or an American or French or German visitor is slain. Then they come and ask embarrassing questions. If they're notified, that is. Sometimes a man with a fat bankroll will disappear here and nobody knows a thing about him. Nobody even saw him. You understand?"

I thought about that for a time as my evening pumps made hollow sounds on the cobblestones. If what Derek said was true, we were in luck. The proprietors of the Blue Goose would wrap what was left of my quarry in canvas, fasten rocks to it, and let it drop into the waters of Victoria Harbor. Or maybe they'd go out to the South China Sea where there was no chance of divers locating the body.

I felt very safe, all of a sudden.

When I said as much to Derek, he growled, "Maybe not so safe. We're being followed—no! Don't turn around. I don't think it's anybody from the Blue Goose, there are about five of them, young Chinese toughs who prey on rich visitors to the quarter when they think they can get away with it,"

He laughed softly. "They must think us real pigeons, pet. They'll come for me first, probably with leather-covered saps. When they've beaten me unconscious, they'll go to work on you."

"Pleasant place, Hong Kong," I commented wryly.

"Oh, it is—if you keep to the right places. But the Chinese quarter after dark is very dangerous. All right, now. Let's consider tactics. How'll we do this? Want to pull the guns?"

I eyed his big bulk. "You any good with your fists?"

"Rather."

"Good. Let them move in on you. I'll take 'em from the flank."

It was his turn to stare at me; somewhat dubiously, I thought. "You really any good at karate or judo?

"You'll find out," I replied smugly.

Another idea was coming to me. These Chinese toughs might be a blessing in disguise. So I slowed my steps, just sauntering along, but I dug that camera compact Derek had given me out of my handbag and opened it. I lifted it, studied the mirror.

"They're about twenty feet away," I breathed.

"They'll make a rush. We'll hear it."

It happened as he said. We heard feet pound the cobblestones suddenly, and just as suddenly, almost as if we'd trained for the moment, Derek and I sprang apart and whirled.

Our movement surprised them. They must have figured that two foreigners, a flabby man and a nervous woman, wouldn't put up much of a fight. Derek Guyfford was big, but these young toughs believed that odds of five to one gave them any advantage they needed.

They moved toward Derek, every last one. They thought I, being a female, was no danger to them. They came in with leather-encased saps held high, padding on slippered feet. I took a couple of steps forward, grabbed the wrist of one, twisted it sideways toward me, and bent down. The tough let out a surprised squawk as he went up into the air and came down hard on the cobblestones.

I yanked the sap from his fingers and in a back-hand blow, slammed it against his forehead. He lost all interest in the proceedings. I whirled.

Derek was boxing, dancing backwards, stabbing with his fists as they sought to close in on him. One tough lost patience, sprang. He caught Derek's fist against his nose, was bowled over.

I wasted no time in watching. I came up from behind a man, drove the sap I held against the back of his head. He pitched headlong. One of the two remaining men turned toward me, eyes going wide at the sight of the billy in my fingers. Then he saw his fallen companions.

Derek had only one opponent, now. He ducked under the swing of the club, he brought a huge fist into his opponent's solar plexus. The youth doubled up, retching. At the same time, the Englishman yanked the sap from him and beat him over the head with it. The man dropped and lay motionless.

My own opponent decided the odds were too much for him. He turned and tried to run, but I was having none of it. I went after him, blue velvet slacks flashing in the moonlight, my disced evening jacket clinking faintly.

When we were twenty feet away from the Englishman, my antagonist turned. I don't think he'd seen what I had done to two of his fellows. He came for me with the sap.

I am an expert in Burmese boxing, in which almost anything goes. I let him come closer, then lashed out with my right foot. The evening pump caught him in the breadbasket. He doubled up. I almost fell down from the force of his cannonballing into me, but I held my balance long enough to swing my sap for the back of his head. It caught him a good one.

He dropped to his knees, rolled over.

Derek came running up, his handsome face split with a grin. "I take back all my doubts, pet. You're a hellcat in high heels."

I brought out the Savage, wiped it off with a perfumed handkerchief, then pushed it into the tough's back pocket. Derek whistled soundlessly, eyes round.

"Getting rid of the evidence," I told him. "Now if they go hunting for the murder weapon, they'll arrest this one for the job."

"You think like a criminal," he admired.

"When I'm on a job, I am a criminal, in a way," I told him. My fingers pushed the sap inside my handbag. "I owe Kim Chow for a gun. I'll see that N.Y.M.P.H.O. pays him."

Derek gestured. "Don't worry, ducks. Kim Chow will put it on his bill. Now let's get the hell out of here."

We ran now, lightly and without undue noise, until we were at the ladder steps. We paused to stare back the way we'd come. Except for the five men lying where they'd fallen, the narrow street was empty. We ran down the ladder steps.

The Austin was where we'd left it. I slid in, so did the Englishman. He turned the ignition, the motor purred to life. The car began to move back the way it had come.

Derek dropped me off at the hotel. I staggered through the lobby to the elevator, made it upstairs and into my room. I yanked off the disced jacket, pushed down the slacks. I slid my tired body between the sheets and tried to get some shuteye.

Sleep was a long time coming. I thought about the other two Mafia buttons I was to execute, and wondered how in hell I was going to stop them from contacting the Chinese tongs. Also, where in hell I'd find them. They had a long head start.

Even if I did manage to catch up to them, maybe my bullets would stop them but not the tong machinery which would find a way to contact other Mafia members. It was a tough, almost an impossible situation. Say for the sake of argument, I did actually kill them. Would I get to them in time? It was not a pleasant prospect. I don't like to fail at a job.

My tired body took over after a time. I slept.

A knock on the suite door woke me to morning sunlight turning my hotel bedroom into a golden glory. I mumbled something about waiting, slid out of the bed and groped for a robe.

Derek Guyfford was in the hall, grinning.

"Don't you ever sleep?" I groused.

"Plenty of time for rest in China, pet. Nothing to do there when the sun goes down except sleep. You eaten yet? No? I'll order from room service. Things I want to talk over with you, in private."

I eyed him suspiciously. He seemed vaguely pre-occupied, and the thought touched my mind that maybe he wanted to change his and back out of our arrangement.

He lit an Erik after ordering ham and scrambled eggs and two pots of coffee over the phone. He draped his bulk in an easychair and studied me as I came out of the bedroom clad in a jersey pullover and slacks.

"Actually," he said as openers. "I have three reasons for going into Red China."

My rump wriggled into a sofa cushion as I asked, "And what are they?"

"First and foremost, since I'm drawing pay from N.Y.M.P.H.O., I'm to be your guide to get you to the two men you intend to kill. Secondly, which is my excuse for getting us passports into Red China, I'm going to take pictures for a book I'm doing about conditions in the mainland today."

"Now we get to the nitty gritty, the real reason," I muttered. "What is it?"

He drew a deep lungful of smoke from his Erik,

and leaned forward. "You ever hear of the Boxer rebellion?"

I frowned. "Seems to me it had something to do with some kind of fighting between British and American and German troops with the Chinese. Back around the turn of the century."

"Right on target. The date was 1900, and the Chinese peasant dissatisfaction with famine and drought exploded into an armed uprising against the foreigners in China. These foreigners were the missionaries who had been allowed in following the Opium War of 1839, which lasted until 1842 when the Chinese surrendered.

"Now this dissatisfaction with their living conditions caused the peasantry to take up arms against the missionaries. They were the scapegoats. The old Empress Dowager looked on complacently, made no attempt to stop them. They got the name Boxers from some sort of secret society. Personally, I think it was a tong thing. As will become clear, perhaps, a little later.

"Of course, the western world was shocked.

"Then the Chinese Boxers, helped by the Imperial armies of the Empress Dowager, attacked the legation compound at Peking. For fifty-five days, these people—British and American, for the most part—fought for their lives.

"Meanwhile, the western world was getting together a relief column. Eight nations—England, the

United States, Austria, Japan, Russia, Germany, Italy and France—sent soldiers. They landed at Taku in the gulf of Chihli and marched overland. They were attacked by the Boxers, they fell back for more reinforcements and then moved through Tientsin to Yangtsun and on to Peking.

"They figured everybody in the foreign quarter would be dead, of course. But there were survivors, and these were freed. With a single cannon of French make, on an Italian gun-mount, using Russian ammunition and sighted by an American marine, they had defended themselves quite ably. They had small arms, too, naturally.

"Now comes the most interesting part of the whole story. To me, at least. In those days Peking was known as the Forbidden City. Nobody could even ride a horse inside its walls without a special dispensation from the Dowager Empress. Whether or not this was because there were treasures beyond price in Peking or not, nobody knows. At any rate, once the Chinese surrendered, the looting began.

"The soldiers from those eight nations took part in the looting, which was natural enough, I suppose. But a great deal of the looting was done by the Chinese. The Boxers? The tong men? Who knows? I believe, from the studies I've been able to make, that the tongs did their share of the stealing.

"And they hid their treasures where nobody could find them."

Derek Guyfford leaned back in his chair, crossed his legs. Pressing his fingertips together, he stared at the ceiling, head tilted to one side.

"Have you any idea, ducks, how much that particular treasure would be worth? There are said to be paintings by such renowned Chinese masters as Liang K'ai and Chou Fang. There are diamonds as big as walnuts, emeralds as large as pecans, rubies the color of rich blood and beyond price. There is gold from the days of Kublai Khan. I talked with a Triad gangster in Hong Kong about a month ago—

"Oh! A Triad gangster is the Hong Kong equivalent of a tong hatchetman. I'm positive they have ties with the secret tong societies on the mainland. At least, my informant told me as much. This informer said that the tong leaders value that hidden treasure as worth a billion dollars on the open market. Always assuming they can find a buyer."

I swallowed hard, sitting bolt upright on the sofa.

"A b-billion dollars! That's a lot of bread!"

"It's a conservative estimate. What would the Metropolitan Museum pay for—say, a dozen Mongol banners known to have been carried into battle by the regiments—the *tumans*—of Genghis Khan? A sword borne by that conqueror, an ivory saddle he sat on, his own horsetail banner. What price such things? Oriental scholars would go mad over them.

"Imagine, if you can, the loot Genghis Khan must have picked up when he overcame an entire continent! Jewels beyond price, hidden away for centuries. Scrolls that might give us an insight as to now-blank periods of history. Remember, Kublai Khan was a grandson of Genghis. He would have stored these treasures in his palace. They would have been part of the heritage of succeeding Chinese emperors and empresses. And there they lay, ducks, ready for the taking of any lightfingered tong man who didn't have to worry about the Empress Dowager torturing him to death.

"The Empress Dowager was a prisoner. They caught her trying to escape Peking and the international army in a peasant's cart, in peasant clothes. She couldn't so much as slap his fingers.

"And so the tong men—knowing far better than any soldier who might come seeking goodies to take home with him the value of those treasures—were the real profiteers. They knew where to put their grubby little paws on works of art, on gems worth a kingdom, on antique swords and weapons, on banners beyond price.

"The tongs have these things hidden away, today.

"And I'm going after them."

I sat speechless. I was seeing another facet of this Englishman, that had been hidden away from me before now. Oh, I didn't blame him for his greed; the tongs had no better title to it than he; they had taken it by stealth, and if he could get it away from them by stealth, the more power to him.

"Where's all this wealth hidden?"

Derek waved a finger at me. "Now, now. I'm not going to tell you. Not yet, at any rate. You can grab a jewel or two if you're so minded, when we get to where it's at. But for now, I keep what I know to my-self."

My shoulders lifted and fell. "Fair enough. I don't mean to pry. If you can smuggle a fortune out of the Chinese mainland, you're welcome to it. Me, I have a job to do."

"Then we'd better get cracking on it." His hand went into his pocket, came out with a passport that he tossed to me. "Your boys gave me some help with this. That's your visa, ducks. I have my own. Check it."

I could have asked for a better picture, maybe, but the passport itself was in order. I slipped it into my handbag alongside the leather-covered sap I'd taken from that attacker last night and the compact camera Derek had given me.

"Okay. What's the first thing we do?"

"Make for Lo Wu on the western side of the New Territories. Lo Wu is the overlook into Red China, which is right across the border. There we take a train—the same train that brings the Red Chinese to Hong Kong and which is normally forbidden to visi-tors. However, I've arranged transportation on it. I suppose because Mao Tse-tung has relaxed the Bamboo Curtain regulations enough to permit me to enter and take the pictures he wants taken."

"Sounds like a stone groove."

His eyebrows lifted quizzically. "I don't quite understand the patois, ducks. But I gather from your tone of voice that you're being sarcastic."

I laughed, "At least, we don't have to walk."

My bags were ready, we called for a bellboy, and when my breakfast wagon arrived, I ate, with Derek joining me in a pot of coffee. As the bellboy took away the luggage, Derek was careful to say nothing to arouse suspicion. We spoke about our coming trip, how excited we were, how grateful to the Red Chinese authorities for giving us the chance to see the mainland. For propaganda purposes, understand, in case the bellboy was a spy of sorts.

Then we were on our way.

Derek Guyfford dipped into his expense account and hired a taxi to drive us to Lo Wu. It was a pleasant ride, the day was sunny and warm, and the streets of Kowloon were crowded with people and other taxis, with bicyclists and with tourists. Derek explained that we might have caught the train at the Sheung Shui station, the first stop inside the New Territories after Lo Wu, but that La Wu was a border stop and arrangements had been made with the Red Chinese border guards to see us on the train. Normally this train will not take passengers on its way back into mainland China; we were to be the exceptions.

We arrived at Lo Wu in plenty of time to catch the train. We sauntered past the little park and the tile-roofed buildings to step out along the railed walkway which served as a lookout spot into Red China. It was an idyllic setting, with the Sham Chun river glistening in the sunlight as if coated with diamonds and beyond it the vast stretch of fertile valley and a range of mountains smothered in haze.

Derek took a few snaps, I oohed and aahed at the scenery, and a couple of border guards watched us from a distance. With their eyes on us, I got a sample of the surveillance we were going to undergo in China proper. A little chill ran down my spine, but Derek paid no heed.

A train whistle roused us.

A big Diesel engine drawing a lot of cars behind it came gliding up to the tiny station. We beat feet toward it. The border guards were there to ask for our passports after my Englishman identified us. A swift perusal of the passport, of our equipment, and the Chinese were all smiles. They didn't ask to examine my handbag, and they let Derek keep the Webley, which he had inside one of his valises.

"No need that," said the guards captain, gesturing at the gun.

Derek shrugged elaborately. "It's just for show, unless I meet some bandits. I've heard a lot about Chinese bandits, you know."

The officer looked shocked, began to protest vehemently that under the glorious reign of the saintly Mao Tse-tung, there were no bandits anywhere in Red China. Then he saw Derek's twinkling eyes and paused. He began to laugh, shaking his head at the good joke.

"You keep gun. You see bandits, you shoot," the captain said, and howled.

Always leave 'em laughing.

The train was quite comfortable, to my surprise. I'd thought I was going to ride on something between the Toonerville Trolley and the local to Podunk. I was given a small stateroom, so was Derek. Since we were the only passengers outside some guards who were going inland, relieved of their posts for a while, the train was all ours.

I made my stateroom comfortable, then sauntered over to visit Derek. He was stretched out in the lone easychair of his stateroom, chatting in Chinese to two grinning guards. They laughed hilariously, from time to time, so I figured he was telling them dirty jokes. Nothing like a joke or two to ease tensions. From the way the two men glanced slyly at me, I wondered if the jokes were on me.

They left, after a time.

"Just checking with them to make sure there was food on board."

"And is there?"

"Oh, yes. One thing I'll say about the Commies. If they want to impress you, they'll spare no expense.

They even have a chef here, to prepare our meals."

I stirred restlessly. "How come the Mafia boys could fly and we have to take the train? It gives them a big head start."

"They made a deal, too. Unfortunately for us, I made our deal before I knew about theirs. You see, there's not supposed to be any rush about our picture taking. A long, slow journey here and there in Red China. The tongs have seen to it that your quarry got out of Hong Kong fast, just in case an extradition order might come through.

"Still, I wouldn't worry, pet."

I eyeballed him doubtfully. "Oh? Why not?"

Derek winked. "I have friends here and there in China. Now, go and read a book or something. I'm tired, I need some shut-eye."

At the door, I paused. "You talk an awful lot like an American, Derek."

"Mother was American. I've spent—oh, a lot of time, stateside. Picked up the idiom, you know. I like the way Americans talk. It's very colorful." He added wryly, "Sometimes it's so colorful, I haven't the faintest idea what they're talking about."

I went out and let him sleep.

The trip was very boring. I did spend a lot of time at the window, admiring the scenery, however. We went north to the town of Cham Shun, then paralleled the river for a time before we finally swung north and west toward Chuchou, where we would transfer to another train that would take us into Chungking. The Diesel-powered engine made damn good time, we must have buzzed along at eighty miles an hour or better, but it was going to be a long pull.

I settled snugly into the chair, curled up and went to sleep. I am very much like a cat; whenever I want to sleep, I can. Naturally, this gives me the energy to do the fighting or the lovemaking which is so very much a part of my job.

I woke, stared out at broad rice fields with Chinese workers, men and women, standing in the shallow water that flooded the fields, working with their hands. There are so many Chinese, so many eager hands to do the work, that sophisticated machinery would be very much out of place. Besides, it would spoil the scenery.

I turned over, wriggled a little, slept again.

Derek woke me, grinning from ear to ear, the baboon.

"Come on, pet. Time to eat."

"Mmmmm. . . ."

We ate chicken and rice, drank tea. We played some gin rummy, we read the books we had brought along. We took catnaps. We spent time staring out at the land through which we were moving. It was very boring.

All I could think of was that those Mafia buttons were long since in Chungking and meeting with the

Chinese tong leaders. Or they could be anywhere in this vast countryside, lost in one of the cities, safely hidden from me. It was even worse than finding a needle in a haystack; the needle never moves around on you.

I decided that I was never going to catch up to them. They were long gone. I might just as well relax and enjoy the sights which I would be helping Derek Guyfford photograph. In a way, this would be the easiest job I'd ever had! Little did I know.

I made Derek give me a few lessons in Chinese. I'd done some studying of the language, of course, every N.Y.M.P.H.O. agent gets a quick study course of most of the major languages of the world, and by this I mean French, German, Spanish, Italian, Russian and Chinese. There are courses in Turkish and Arabic also, but I'd skipped these. A girl can study only so much.

So Derek Guyfford was my one-man refresher course.

There was nothing else to do, and the way was long and tiresome all those many miles to Chungking. I made a good pupil because I was interested in learning. If some Red Chinese guard told me to halt I wanted to make sure I knew he wasn't just whispering love words.

During the Sino-Japanese war, Chungking had the dubious distinction of being the most bombed Chinese city. It used two big red paper balls to sound the air raid alarm, when its half million population ran for the caves and bomb shelters in the sandstone ridge on which it is built. One of those tunnels held close to twenty thousand people. Today, of course, Chungking is one of the more important cities of the country.

It is built on the Yangtze river, at one time it was the capital of Free China. The approaches I found lovely, with high hills all around it and the eternal rice paddies sweeping across a vast land under a blue sky in which white clouds lazily floated. It was a very pleasant sight.

Derek was at my elbow watching the workers in the rice fields. "Poor devils," he said softly.

"They seem happy to me," I remarked.

"Ducks, you don't know the way Red China functions. Nobody does, in the western world. Every man, woman and child in China stays where he or she is put. There's no moving around, the way we do. Each man has his job, he can't leave it without a lot of red tape and government suspicion. They've learned it's better to get along on the wages they're paid—seventy yuans or about twenty-five American dollars, on the average—than to make waves. It's an existence, unless they're in the upper echelon. Which isn't much better, to my way of thinking. Everyone and everything is regimented. If it weren't, communist China could never survive."

I remembered the Red Guards, the fighting peasants, the rebellions that had flared up, here and there in this land over the past nine or ten years. Slowly but inexorably, the government ground out rebellion, stifled free thought, crunched everyone into a pattern.

I sighed. "It seems a shame. China has such a wonderful tradition, a history of scholars and artists."

"They still have them, but they do what the government tells them to do, the way they do in Russia. You can have Communism, ducks. I'll take capitalism and the free life."

The train was gliding into the city outskirts. I leaned back, looked at Derek. "What's the first thing on the agenda?"

"We have accommodations at the Kialing House, which is a very nice hotel for Red Chinese dignitaries and visiting foreigners like us." He hesitated a moment, then added, "I have a friend waiting for us at the Kialing House."

"If these people are so regimented that they're afraid to move about, what good can your friend do?"

"When the government winks an eye, no man sees a thing. It is the wish of the Red Chinese government that I take these pictures, that the book be published so that the western world can see the great advances made by Red China under the guidance of Mao Tse-tung. In short, it will be propaganda."

"How does the government regard the tongs?"

"It doesn't know about them. Officially, that is. But I have more than a sneaking suspicion that it winks an eye—as long as the tongs behave themselves and work for the betterment of the Chinese People's Republic. This is the way I think."

"Hmmmm. And if it learned the tongs want to ally themselves with the Mafia?"

"All hell could break loose. And burn us up, too. So keep cool, ducks. Let daddy Derek carry the ball."

At the train station, we made our way through throngs of merchants offering everything for sale from New Year's masks to newly plucked chickens, toward a dragon gate painted in vivid reds and blues. A young man in a black linen suit was waiting patiently. I saw his face light up at sight of the big Englishman, he took a few steps forward and held out his hand.

"*Ho ts'ai*," he cried. "I am glad seeing you, sir."

"Wing Dock, by all that's holy," exclaimed Derek and grasped the other's hand, pumping it. "Don't tell me you're to be our guide?"

Wing Dock bowed. "Is so." His black eyes touched me. "This the lady helper?"

I held out my hand, too. I said in Chinese, haltingly. "I'm glad to know you."

With that politeness for which the Chinese are noted, he bowed and said slowly in his own language, "I want to welcome you to the Peoples' Republic, Miss Delight, on behalf of all my people."

With his help, there was no trouble getting our bags through the dragon gate, where an official was placed to keep an eye on newcomers. Not foreigners, there are practically no foreigners in China. But from time to time, people from one province will travel to another—with the proper orders and permission, if they know what's good for them—and there are always government representatives to see that they have the right orders.

We entered a taxi, set off for the Kialing House.

Wing Dock said softly, "Two men come Chungking. White men, like you. Come make trade agreements."

"And you believe them?" Derek answered.

The Chinaman shrugged. "Not for me to believe, not believe. I take orders, follow them." He pursed his lips, added, "They guests of Gum Dow. Gum Dow high official in Chinese Party."

"Of course. But I'd appreciate it if you'd let us know where they're staying in Chungking."

Wing Dock bowed slightly. "It be done."

The Kialing House is not a new establishment. It was used before and during the Sino-Japanese war to house foreigners, and I guess it still functioned in that capacity. Chinese travellers made up the vast bulk of its guest list, of course, but I saw a French newsman and a couple of Albanians while we were there.

The Mafia boys were staying with Gum Dow, we were informed. One of Wing Dock's men was watching it, and would report to us. Meanwhile, we could wash up and take a nap, and begin our photography work before the sun went down.

We went about our business as was to become our custom. With Derek laden with three or four cameras, with me trailing after him, we made our way up and down streets, always taking pictures when Wing Dock suggested it. He had his duty to perform, that of guide; it was only a secondary duty he was performing, letting us know about the Mafia buttons.

Two days later we were still tramping the streets taking photos of the happily smiling people, of stores with plenty of food in evidence, dressed ducks, hams, chickens, bags of oranges and suchlike, which was to impress the outside world, I felt sure. Wing Dock was a pleasant companion, he and Derek held long talks in Chinese, of which I picked up a few words now and then.

For the most part, I was bored silly. I trailed after them like a hound trained to heel. I never used the compact camera, not once. Inside me, I was worried. Suppose the Mafia musclemen left Chungking and I never learned about it? I became somewhat irritable.

Derek soothed me, as best he could. "After all, pet, if I don't take these pictures, somebody will get suspicious. And we don't want that, now do we?"

He had a point there. So I went on making like a zombie until one evening, a very excited Wing Dock showed up as we were feasting our faces on Bombay duck and announced that the Mafia buttons were making their move. His man had informed him that a man with a scar on his lower face had taken a taxi to the Golden Cloud House, which was a restaurant, to all intents and purposes.

"There is ballroom in Golden Cloud House," Wing Dock added softly. "Ballroom is part of old bomb shelter."

"And what's in the old bomb shelter?" wondered Derek.

Wing Dock jerked his head at me, muttered some Chinese words. I watched the Englishman's face. A smile fought at the corners of his mouth. He muttered in an aside to me, "He means a bordello, ducks."

He spoke to his informant some more. Then he interpreted, "Wing Dock says that certain highly placed men of government are allowed to frequent these sin parlors. Nobody is supposed to know about them, certainly not the great mass of the people. But they do exist, on a sub rosa plane. Your man is going there for some flesh fun, it seems."

"Then so am I."

Wing Dock was horrified. "No can do. No lady let in!"

I thought a few seconds. "Is there any place I can

buy some makeup? I could tint my skin, fix up my face so I'd look more than a little oriental."

Wing Dock considered me for a long minute. He asked hesitantly, "You are not embarrass go such a place?"

"It's how I make my living. I don't intend to stay there."

The Chinaman nodded slowly. "You come me. I take you place I knowing. Fix you there." When Derek began to rise, Wing Dock raised a hand. "You staying here, please. Must not let you taking picture."

I went with Wing Dock to a taxi and we were driven through the teeming streets and a little back alley to a white-faced building without any signs on it at all. Wing Dock explained that it was a very secret place, he wasn't even sure the Red Chinese big shots knew about it. If they did, they didn't admit it. This made sense to me, since I've found in Communist countries, there are two sets of rules, one for the common man and a completely different one for the hierarchy.

Wing Dock issued me into a cool room, tastefully but simply outfitted, and turned me over to a pretty girl. He explained to her in slow Chinese, so I could follow him, that I was to be made into a yellow blossom, a China doll. A concubine, in other words.

The girl stared at me with big black eyes. There was worry in her expression. Kao Ton said nothing while Wing Dock was there, but when he left, she whispered in my ear, also in slow Chinese, "Is bad place you go. May not come out alive. You listen Kao Ton."

"I can take care of myself," I assured her.

She seemed very gloomy. I reflected that maybe I ought to worry, too. She might know something I didn't, something that might save my life.

Chapter Five

Pretty Kao Ton was a makeup expert. She made me strip naked, filled her palms with some sort of stuff that looked like glue, and began rubbing it all over my body. Her smooth palms rubbed it into my pores, she went over my breasts very carefully, and my belly, my backside and my back. She knelt and ran those syrupy hands up and down my legs, along my inner thighs, into every nook and cranny that would make me into a Chinese girl.

"You not say much," she warned. "You not talking so good the Chinese. Not give anyone anything to ask you questions, about."

She made sense, I decided. She informed me that if I looked shy and timid, I could get away with a lot. Chinese girls are not expected to chatter about world politics and international affairs. They are in the Golden Cloud House for only one purpose.

"You not shy too much?" she asked, eyebrows raised.

"I not shy at all," I grinned.

She nodded, smiling faintly. "I seeing that, way you not blush when I touching you. Is good sign. Know way around."

I stared at my image in the mirror when she was done with me. I was a Chinese girl, for fair. My normally red hair was black as a raven's wing, my skin was a pale gold. Of course, my nipples were brown, my lips red, but this wasn't unusual for a Chinese girl.

"You bigger there," Kao Ton said, pointing at my pubic bush that she had dyed black to match my head hair. I stared down between my sharply nippled breasts at my pubic motte, saw the thick hairs growing. I felt a little different in black hair and yellow skin, it was like a disguise. And it's said that women who wear masks to costume balls where they won't be known, are apt to let the barriers down in their conduct. Not that I needed any such booster to my naturally amoral nature. It just made it easier.

"Let's see yours," I smiled.

Kao Ton giggled and smoothed her palms on the silken sides of her cheong-sam. These Chinese garments are very proper, they cover a girl from ankles to neck, but they are made of thin silk or linen, and they have a lovely habit of clinging to the body that is inside them. Which can be quite revealing when that body is otherwise naked. As was Kao Ton's slender shape, I felt sure.

Her red-nailed fingers gathered the folds of her skirt, raised it. Up it came, revealing handsome golden legs and dimpled knees, somewhat plump thighs. Then her vaginal dimple came into view, deepset and sensual. There were no hairs on its lips, none I could see, anyhow. Above it, on the plumply fleshed mons veneris, there were only a few sparse black hairs.

"You see?" she exclaimed triumphantly.

I saw, all right. The hem of the cheong-sam was up above her cute little bellybutton as she showed her private parts off to me without any shame. Now the Chinese have always been a race that likes its sex fun and games, books like the classic *Ch'in P'ing Mei* prove that, together with some of their erotic paintings done by such masters of the brush as Shih K'o and Chao Meng Fu.

Which was why the enforced celibacy and unnatural prudery of the communist Chinese struck me as a bit off-key. It just wasn't natural. And when human feelings are repressed, they burst at sometime or another in a startling about-face. This could explain such places as the Golden House. The government may have known about it and others like it, but the authorities winked a casual eye.

I put out my hand, ran gentle fingertips through

that sparse pubic growth. Kao Ton giggled shrilly, her thighs opened very slightly, and her black eyes implored me to caress her.

I was ready, willing and able. Kao Ton was a real doll and I can go one way or the other and have myself a ball. So my fingers dipped into her vaginal dimple, slid around it, and downward. They encountered what seemed to be a tiny twig. Well, the old Romans called the female clitoris the *virga*, which means twig. Hers was rather large and thick. I teased it gently.

"Why don't you come along with me?" I coaxed. "We can make the clouds burst for both of us."

The Chinese language is very flowery, quite romantic. The phrase '*wo yai tiu la*' means that the lady or the man is having an orgasm. Its literal translation is, 'My cloud is bursting.' And the way Kao Ton stood with her thighs apart, her lower lip held between her teeth, made me think that maybe her own vaginal cloud was just about to rain down its heavenly dew on my probing fingers.

"I—couldn't," she whimpered. "Is not permit."

"I'll talk to Wing Dock," I breathed.

She had put her own hands on my bare sides, was moving them up to my tumid breasts. Most Chinese ladies have very small titties, I guess my large ones acted as an aphrodisiac to her.

What might have happened between us, did not. There was a knock on the door, Kao Ton jumped back and dropping her cheong-sam hem, whirled to grasp the knob.

Wing Dock entered. His eyes got big at sight of me standing there stark naked. His tongue touched his lips. Then his oriental impassivity came to the fore—along with something else I could see sticking up in his pants leg—as his eyes grew hooded and remote. He bowed to Kao Ton.

"You have done a remarkable job, Kao Ton. I am pleased."

"I did it for the great Mao Tse-tung, our father and helper, Wing Dock. It was my duty and I did the best I could."

Words she spoke out of long habit, nobody but I could know how her little red pussylips must be aching for some amative attention.

"I have an idea," I exclaimed brightly. "Why doesn't Kao Ton come along with me? She can act as interpreter in case somebody says something in Chinese I don't understand."

Wing Dock looked forbidding. "Is not her task, to be concubine. We each have job to do for betterment of the People's Republic, Miss Delight."

I thought fast. "Well, she'd be on hand to make sure my skin didn't blotch or rub off. That's her job, isn't it?"

Wing Dock glanced at the girl. I guess he knew what hardships that enforced no-sex rule puts on young, healthy people. He was looking in her face for an answer to my plea. I stared at her, too. Her pretty features were masklike, but her eyes were saying yes, yes, yes! Wing Dock chuckled.

"I see no harm in it," he declared pontifically, in Chinese, "After all, Kao Ton will be seeing to it that this most important mission of yours achieves success, Miss Delight. If she is willing, let her come."

Kao Ton gurgled happily, then smothered it. Wing Dock turned away so as not to see her face, and lifted his hand to hide a smile. I'll bet the guy would have given an arm and a leg to be able to come with us.

A taxi was waiting for us—one of those China-built cars they call a Shanghai sedan—and we slid into the back seat. Wing Dock sitting between us girls. I was wearing a black linen cheong-sam by this time, ornamented with small red rectangles which were tiny representations of the national flag. They didn't do a thing for the cheong-sam—or for me, either.

We were whisked between bicycles and walking workers across the city. The Golden Cloud House was an old style structure, complete with dragon gate straddling a driveway that led to a covered portico and a three storey building done in the Mandarin style with lots of curving eaves and tiled roofs and moon windows.

It was dark by this time, and we were showed no lights as Wing Dock guided us up the few steps to the front door. A husky Chinese opened the door, let us in. I learned later that Wing Dock posed as a procurer, gathering girls for the Golden Cloud House, in order to act as a spy on its activities. The Golden Cloud House paid him well for each girl, but he never got to keep the money, he turned it over to the People's Republic.

We waited in a hall redolent with incense and perfume, the scent of old wood panelling and cooking food, until a small Chinese man, very old and with a long white beard, came to greet us. His hands were tucked inside the loose sleeves of his Mandarin robe, he was very polite as his eyes under puffy lids glanced at Kao Ton and myself before swinging to Wing Dock.

"You have done well, my friend. I shall put these two to work immediately. You will see Lem Ho, who will have your money for you."

They bowed ceremoniously to each other.

The old man turned, walked away without a glance at us. Wing Dock whispered, "Follow him!" and we did.

"There is a banquet in progress," he murmured as he paused to put a hand on a swinging door covered with red velvet and imitation gold trimming. I wondered if he were high in the councils of a Chinese tong. Sort of like a Mafia don, to be exact.

"We shall enter, but we shall not interrupt what is going on."

Like little sheep, we trailed at his heels.

We found ourselves in what was a magnificent banqueting hall, with tables arranged in a squared U shape, with a lot of room for the performers in the open space. The diners had feasted well on their meal, it had taken a long time to serve because it had been several hours since Wing Dock arrived with the news that one of our Mafia boys was attending it.

Neither Kao Ton nor I gave much more than a single glance at the diners—there were ten of them. I noted—because our eyes went immediately to the naked Chinese wrestler and the little China doll he was bouncing up and down on his upstanding male organ. He was fat, gross, he must have weighed three hundred pounds. I guess he had muscles. but they were hidden under layers of fat. His arms were thicker than my thighs.

Those arms were under the legs of a naked girl who was mewling and sobbing in delight as his arms, plus her bare arms about his thick neck, supported her as he walked around with her. His hands under her buttocks lifted and dropped her again and again. His thick shaft, covered with her love juices, was a glistening bar of flesh pistoning in and out of her.

Kao Ton gurgled. I felt my heart start its phallic pound.

Up and down that girl went, buttocks jellying, like a monkey on a stick. The fat man would lift her almost all the way off him, and he was very large down there, and then take his hands away so suddenly that force of gravity dropped her the full length of his turgid staff.

My eyes moved away from them. I saw a man with a scar at the corner of his mouth that ran to his chin, a man with curling black hair and quite good to look at if you like the dark, swarthy type. He had Mafia written all over him, I can tell them at a look, I've worked against those gangsters so many times.

I wondered what his name might be. He was my quarry, all right. No doubt about it. I also wondered how I was going to kill him, since I had no weapons on me. All I had was my naked body under the linen cheong-sam.

The old man whispered, "Go to the other end of the hall. There you will find other girls. Wait with them until you are told what to do."

I walked with Kao Ton in that little shuffle step she adopted that was a carryover from the days when Chinese women had to walk that way because of their bound and crippled feet. For some reason I can't understand to this day, Chinese lovers thought that small feet were quite erotic, in the olden days. A painting of a nude female foot was thought to be the last word in eroticism. They could look at pictures of a vulva, of bared breasts and buttocks, without a qualm. But a bare foot! Outtasite, man. Just goes to show what queer things we human beings are, I guess.

The shuffle step is a memory of those old days. It wouldn't mean a thing to Scarface, but to the Chinese onlookers, it was really something. I saw them glance away from the performers to stare at Kao Ton and myself.

We took our places with the other girls, each of whom wore the same type garment we did. I must say I filled mine out a little better than the others, my tits were larger and shoved out that linen like big balloons trying to get free of what held them, jouncing up and down. My hips pressed into the thin stuff, the men could see my buttocks wobbling as I walked.

Our eyes were watching the fat man and the small girl whom he was sliding up and down on his manhood. They were nearing the climax of the act, which would take place when the wrestler 'burst his cloud.' The girl had burst her own cumulus a dozen times already, the onlookers could see the fluids along that long male shaft, see a little of it dripping to the floor.

The men watching this performance were in a state of wild delight. Not one of them didn't have a hardon, I'd have bet. And the way Scarface was sliding around in his chair told me he was damn excited.

A voice whispered, "You will go to the diners, when the act is finished. You will sit on their laps, you will accommodate them in whatever way they ask."

I guess by this time the girls were ready for a bout of yin and yang, they could hardly help it after watching the fat man perform. Some of them breathing quite heavily, and I don't except myself. I know Kao Ton was shivering steadily.

My eyes touched the girls. I counted nine, besides Kao Ton and me. I leaned my lips to her ear, breathed, "You stay with me. We'll both work on the man with the scarred face, the foreigner."

She nodded happily.

The fat man was wedging the girl down on him, his hips were pumping, pumping, his head was thrown back and his face was twisted into a mask of absolute joy—the *yin chu yang* of the Chinese—as he held the girl firmly in place. She was shuddering, but she could not move her hips, not with those huge hands holding her. She just sat there and let Nature take its course.

He staggered as he lifted the girl from his manhood. When Kao Ton saw it, she gasped. It was very long, almost nine inches. Now the normal Chinese penis is about five inches in repose, six inches fully extended. No wonder she was so amazed. The man and the girl walked, they did not run, toward us. Tiny lines of tiredness showed in their faces. A thunder of applause followed them every step of the way.

"Go," said a voice.

With soft squeals, the girls ran for the diners. Their cheong-sams fluttered, they ran with little swayings of their hips. They had seen how our shuffle step had won the approbation of the guests, they adopted it. Kao Ton and I made for the man with the scar.

He grinned from ear to ear when he saw that he was getting two girls. It was a compliment to his manhood, I supposed. One girl was not enough for him. I just hoped he could perform to the satisfaction of two girls. I didn't want Kao Ton disappointed on this humping holiday of hers, and of course, I'm a bit selfish that way, myself.

I tilted his head back and gave him a wide-lipped kiss, thrusting my tongue between his lips. I heard a rustle of cloth and Kao Ton dipped out of sight. Scarface grunted, jerked.

Taking my lips away, I saw that Kao Ton was under the table, hidden from view by the long cloth. Only her slim golden hands were visible, grasping and clutching the rigid manhood that was visible now as her fingers were entwined around it, over his pants.

"Jeez,"breathed Scarface.

I lifted my cheong-sam skirt, straddled his hips and climbed onto them. My garment was up to my navel, his eyes were assessing my belly, the thick bush of my black pubic hair, my thighs.

"You're a doll, baby," he grated.

I pretended not to understand his language, *"Ho t'sai!"* I cried, which is a term of approval in Chinese.

A zipper tab rasped. I felt Kao Ton's hand under my buttocks, sliding into his fly. I could visualize that slender hand wrapping its fingers about his organ. Scarface lay back in the chair, completely given over to pleasure. Underneath the table, of course, Kao Ton could see my exposed buttocks and my private parts. An instant later I felt a finger sliding into my vagina. I writhed and panted as it slid around and tapped my clitoral bud.

Scarface grinned up at me. "I told Tommasso to have himself some fun before we got down to business. These Chinks know how to treat a guest, I'll say. But no, Big Tommy can't be bothered. Whatta stupid slob."

I kept a straight face, but I was beginning to see how my role of Chinese concubine who spoke only Chinese, could come in very handy. I tabbed this button as a talker, he liked to rap while he was having his jollies. This suited me to the proverbial tee.

To please him a little more, I raised the cheongsam upward to my armpits. This brought my big breasts into view. He stared at them as they hung naked, quivering, with my nipples stiff and pointed. His tongue came out, ran around his lips.

Behind and below us, Kao Ton was having a time for herself. She was bringing his erection out of his pants, brushing it against my buttocks. I heard her faint giggle. Her hand pushed up my behind, I rose upward on my feet so that she could slide that male shaft directly under my moist vulva.

I sank down an inch, felt his flesh at my girlish opening. I sank down some more, almost lazily. Scarface was groaning, head rammed into the chairback. I leaned to nuzzle a nipple against his mouth. His lips parted, drew in that brown breast tip. He began to nurse on it hungrily.

A little more swiftly, I sank downward. Now he was all the way inside me, held firmly by my constrictor muscles. These muscles can give a girl a good name in the sex line. For an instance, a girl who can use these interior muscles is known as a 'nut cracker,' or as the French phrase it, *casse-noisette*. Among the Arab lands, she is called a *geb-badzeh*, one who clutches, and her favors come very high, indeed. I am told by Mark Condon, who has experienced my own clutchings many times, that it feels as if a soft, wet hand is milking his penis.

I guess Scarface was feeling much the same way because he was groaning, lips twisted loosely in his delight, as my inner self went to work on what it held. A woman doesn't even have to move, except inside her, when she uses the constrictors. But I am of the belief that a man likes to see what is giving him all this pleasure,. I am one with my sister *ghenu-jehs*—wiggler women—in that regard. I put on a show for a guy.

So I did a bump and grind, I writhed into a belly dance, contorting my belly muscles and letting my breasts do a milk shake for his bulging eyeballs. After all, I was going to kill this guy in a little while, so I figured he might as well die happy. I'm a very altrustic person, this way.

I was sliding around, sticking out my belly at him and withdrawing it, leaning forward to slap my tits against his face, to dip a nipple between his lips, when I felt Kao Ton slide her hand around to my mons veneris. I was having a ball, really, but when I felt her fingers slide over my outthrust clitoral bud, I really hit the fluttering fan.

She tickled and teased my twig, she toyed with it. At the same time I felt her tongue sliding over my buttocks and dipping into the crease. I whooped and jounced, pounding myself down on the phallic peg I was riding for all I was worth, then rising upward.

"*Lento, lento,*" he panted, grabbing my hips.

In another moment he was going to burst his cloud for fair.

I took pity on him. I slowed down, I just sat on him and let Kao Ton tease me with her tongue and fingers. I burst my own cloud a number of times, I was off in seventh heaven. And when I felt Scarface swelling inside me, I reached down behind me to catch his testicles in a hand and give them a squeeze.

The pain flared into his eyes.

His hand came up. I think he would have hit me

except that he remembered suddenly that he was in a foreign land and a Chinese girl—or so he believed —was pumping up and down on him. He gave me a wry grin.

"Sorry about that, lady," he growled. "I guess you know your business pretty good. I was about to spend all over the place, but you stopped that and now I can go on."

His hands slid up and down my bare thighs, then moved up under my breasts. He cupped them in his palms, bounced them. They jellied up and down, he stared at them with wide eyes and open mouth. I don't know for sure whether Scarface was a tit man but he sure ogled my mammaries. He was still inside me and strong as ever.

I made a few movements with my pelvis.

Behind me, kneeling on the floor, I felt Kao Ton must be undergoing some amoral agonies right about now. She'd been teasing the two of us for a long time, so I figured she ought to be sitting where I was, straddling Scarface's thighs.

I lifted a leg, started to dismount.

"Hey, doll. Stay put!" howled Scarface.

It was a bit of a strain on me, not to be able to talk, but since I didn't want him to know I under-stood English, and because he certainly didn't savvy even my poor brand of Chinese, I lifted the flap of the tablecloth so he could see Kao Ton.

He grinned, "How about that! Your little China

doll partner wants in on the action, too. Why not, kiddo? Go ahead. Let her take your place."

I stared at him as if I couldn't understand him. He laughed, slapped my hip, lifted my leg. I laughed, dismounted, and told Kao Ton in what was probably awful Chinese to put her yin on his yang.

She nodded happily, came out from under the table. I took her place, kneeling before his legs as she rose up, flung a leg over him and started to sit down. She put her hand there to hold him steady as she zeroed on him. Then she sank down until his manhood was out of view.

I watched her private parts, void of any hair except for that tiny little beard on her mons veneris, lift and fall. I put my fingers under his hairy testicles, played at spiders' legs on them. He started to moan.

Kao Ton's golden buttocks were shaking and jiggling right before my eyes, too, but I paid no never mind to them. I was busy thinking. I knew damn well I couldn't execute Scarface in this dining room, not with his fellow diners and diddlers looking on.

We needed privacy.

In Chinese, I whispered up to Kao Ton to ask if we couldn't have a private room. She was a sharp girl, she knew she just couldn't come out with it. So she practised her Americanese on the Mafia button.

"Is good, hey not?" she panted.

"You speak English, hey, kiddo? Maybe not so

good, but I can understand ya. That other one, guess all she talks is Chinee, hey?"

"She not know how."

"That don't make no difference to me. Long as you do. Keep goin', kiddo. You sure are nice and tight. Like the other one. I like you both."

"Likee us all night?"

"That sure is a great idea. Sure I would. You think you can arrange it? I got to travel to Soochow to-morrow. It's gonna be a long trip in that train, and I won't be able to get no nookie until we get to Soochow. So go ahead, ask."

Kao Ton spoke rapid Chinese for a few seconds.

I heard halting footsteps, realized the old man had drawn near. He said some gibberish the main point of which was that Scarface—the name he mentioned was Cesare Iannotto—was their honored guest, nothing was too good for him and if he wished to enjoy the embraces of two lovely girls in a private room, it was ready for him.

"Can do," Kao Ton said, giving a naughty wriggle of her hips. "Can go now, if wanting."

I had to pretend not to know what was going on, so when Kao Ton got off that upstanding male shaft, I grabbed it with both hands.

"Easy, kiddo, go easy," said Cesare Iannotto, laughing, trying to free himself. "We're goin' up-stairs, the three of us. We're going to have some more fun, you bet." Then: "Crissakes, babe—tell her to let go."

Kao Ton, her black eyes sparkling with laughter, shook a finger at me and told me to release the man at once, that we were going to another room with him where I would have all the screwing I wanted. This was in impeccable Chinese I guess, because all the diners and their girl friends were laughing and making comments to each other on the ways of foreigners. Kao Ton assisted me to get to my feet. As my eyes swept the room I saw that a lot of assorted coupling was going on around us.

One man who looked like a fat Buddha, his skin sleek and shiny, had a girl resting on his organ and leaning her elbows on the table before her. Naturally, her bare behind was facing him, and the muscles in her legs bulged and relaxed as she raised and lowered herself slowly. Another girl was crouched between the widespread legs of a tall, lean man, feasting on the membrum she held between her big lips. A third was seated on the table as her fellow fish lover stood between her upheld legs and worked himself in and out of her vagina.

Kao Ton caught me by the hand, brought me at a shuffle-footed trot behind Scarface who had managed to put away the long evidence of his fleshy desires and was casually sauntering to a narrow door held open for him by the old man.

It was Kao Ton who took over once we'd passed through the doorway. Her slim legs took us to the next floor and into a room fitted with a bed, a chair. and a washstand. Cesare Iannotto came in, closed the door, and made a quick search of the room. He was looking for bugs, and I don't mean the kind that crawl. Satisfied, he started to undress.

I ran to help him.

He was naked except for his shorts which I was sliding down, going on one knee to do it, when Kao Ton came up behind me. She asked, "You like seeing us put on girlie show, hey? You like seeing us make love?"

"I sure would, babe, but I got the hots already."

Indeed he did have the hots, as we both saw when the shorts came down. His prong leaped into view and throbbed, quivering as though balanced on springs. I put a hand around it, squeezed.

Kao Ton said, "I takee first!"

I made believe I didn't hear her, let her shove me out of the way. She pushed the Mafia button down on the bed and crawled over him, squatting with her hairless genitals inches from his mouth.

"Make Kao Ton feeling good," she begged.

Iannotto was willing. His hands came up to her thighs, widened them and drew her downward so she crouched on hands and toes, legs spread before his face. He brought her closer, began to lick at those scarlet, moist folds. Kao Ton wailed softly, head thrown back, eyes closed. She shook and quivered, and when I caught her dangling breasts in my hands and shook them gently, she howled.

My own privacies were moist and throbbing, it was a pleasant sight indeed to see Kao Ton enjoying this form of lovemaking that was old when the men of Nola practiced it on Crispa. In ancient times, the women of Oscanus in Italy were noted for their addiction to this pleasure, as in more modern times the women of certain provinces of India were so famed.

I glanced at Scarface, saw his male spear lifted long and thick from his hairy loins. The thought touched my mind that if he were sexually exhausted, he would be that much easier to kill. If I just stood here like a bump on a log, nothing would be accomplished in that direction.

So I clambered up on the bed, turned around so my backside brushed Kao Ton's shaking buttocks, and catching that love lance between my fingers, sat my most sensitive self down on it. It sank deep, I wanted to drain him of all energy. I rested a moment, crouched on hands and feet in the approved frog-hop posture, then rose upward.

Kao Ton's genital folds muffled his groan, but I could hear it. Up and down, around and around in a kind of broomstick bellydance went my hips. Don't get me wrong, I was having a lot of fun. What girl wouldn't, in such a position? But my main concern was to tire Cesare Iannotto out, to make him sleep the slumber of the exhausted.

I lazed through my motions, I speeded them up. I kept him on the *quivive*, in a manner of speaking. He was a lighted firecracker ready to blow up, but Kao Ton and I kept his fuse burning—and I do mean burning!—for long, long minutes.

The boy had staying power. I grant him that. But eventually something had to give.

And Scarface gave, shuddering and shaking, hips lifting to hold himself in me as he wept those seminal tears which the French so aptly name *jus de couillon*. He was sobbing in his delight, but soft flesh kept those sounds to a very minimum.

Then he was pushing her away, saying, "Let me get my breath, girls. *Marrone!* That was really something."

He lay, naked, inert, on the bed as Kao Ton crawled off him. I followed her example, glancing back at him. His eyes were closed, but his chest rose and fell as he breathed in and out. He didn't look quite tired enough to me.

My eyes glanced at a pillow longingly. To grab it, hold it over his face until he stopped breathing was a very tempting idea, but he might push the pillow away and yell and there I'd be in a den of tong thieves, all alone.

No, no. We had to exhaust him some more.

So I ran for the bathroom with Kao Ton at my heels. There was no shower, no bathtub here, but there was a washstand with some towels. We had to make do, wiping off the lovesweat and the love tears, making ourselves presentable again.

"Hey," yelled Cesare Iannotto after a time. "Where are you dames?"

Towelling our naked flesh dry, our hair hanging down in what I thought might be a very tempting sight, we moved from the bathroom. Scarface was sitting on the edge of the bed, grinning. To judge by the sight of his limp but long male appendage, he was getting in the mood for another bout of sheet sex.

Kao Ton grinned wickedly, slid behind me, plastering her smooth belly and her sparsely haired mons veneris to my buttocks, reached up and caught my breasts. She toyed with them, palms sliding over those big mounds, she cupped and bounced them up and down. A hand slid down to my hairy motte, dipped inside the lips of my love dimple. In seconds she had found my clitoris, was teasing it.

Scarface watched all this with big eyes.

"Come on, come on, stop foolin' around. Get over here on the bed with me."

We pretended we didn't understand him. I turned in Kao Ton's arms, kissed her pouting mouth with open lips. Our breasts mashed, our thighs rubbed together. The girl was gradually pushing me toward the bed. Kao Ton was lowering her head, kissing my swollen nipples, licking my breasts. I was caressing her smooth buttocks with both hands, letting sensuousness wash over me.

Scarface was licking his lips, eyeing our nude bodies. His manhood was up and quivering for attention, but we girls ignored it. Let the bastard suffer.

We fell on our sides on the mattress, crawled up onto it, and then I was on my back and Kao Ton was on top of me, gently rubbing her mons veneris into my own, kissing my lips, her tongue deep in my mouth. We fondled each other, we put hands between each other's thighs, caressed the liquid folds gaping for those touches. We panted like wheezy bellows.

Iannotto was dancing around, trying to get at us.

"Hold still, damn you!" he'd growl, and lunge at Kao Ton whose backside and slightly parted thighs were an open invitation to his maleness.

We would shift position, roll over on our sides so he'd be left kneeling without any place to bury his need. I think there was a touch of sadism in both us girls at the moment, we were having too good a time to bother about him.

The Chinese girl was slithering around now, sliding her kisses from my throat to my breasts, to my soft, heaving belly—and lower. Her lips nuzzled my pubic hairs. I felt the pull of her hands on my inner thighs to part them.

Then her mouth was there where I needed it, her tongue was a paintbrush dipped in utter ecstacy, moving, laving, tapping. I wailed, I sobbed, my head swung like the weight of a pendulum back and forth, back and forth.

I heard bedsprings creak, and paid no attention.

Then Kao Ton jerked and my eyes opened.

Scarface was kneeling behind her, to one side of me, grasping her buttocks and half lifting her, his rod rigid and demanding, an angry red. I watched almost unwillingly, but I was happy for Kao Ton. Now she would be pleased, as well as I.

He thrust, her face bumped my genitals, then he began to move in and out of her. I could hear the slurping sounds of their genitals but paid no attention because Kao Ton had resumed her gentle nursing on my own fevered folds and was bringing me that delight the Chinese call *yen*. My fists beat the bedcovers, my head was a living metronome. My hips rose and fell.

A knock sounded on the door.

Scarface shouted, "Go away, goddamit!"

And Kao Ton raised her face to cry out, "*Kung hsi!* What a time to knock. Go away, stupid one!" Me, I didn't say a thing.

Then we heard footsteps, receding.

Kao Ton lowered her head, her lips caught my genital folds.

And Scarface began pumping his hips all over again.

I couldn't see the Chinese girl's face, it was buried

out of sight between my thighs, and so I could scarcely tell her to prolong this sweet agony, this sharing of the *fang shu*. I wanted desperately for Cesare Iannotto to become so tired, so weary, that he would just fall over in a dead sleep after he finally burst his cloud inside Kao Ton! Yet I could say nothing without warning him.

And so we worked on, Kao Ton with her lips, Scarface with his maleness. I was getting tired myself, to tell the truth, and the ironic thought came into my mind that maybe I wouldn't have the strength to wield that pillow, to hold it firmly in place while the Mafia button kicked out his life under it.

I couldn't push Kao Ton away, to rest.

The thrills and chills her lips and tongue were feeding my pussylips and my hot little *virga* were too wildly exciting to stop. My hands were too wildly exciting to stop. My hands were clinging to the coverlets, clutching them as a drowning man might cling to a bit of driftwood.

I was up there with Ho Tei, the Chinese god of joy.

My flesh rippled and bounced in utter delight. I felt as though I lived only between my thighs, where Kao Ton feasted. I didn't care if I ever killed Cesare Iannotto. I floated in ecstacy, with my 'flower heart' wet and loose, demanding more and more of this pleasure.

Then Scarface bellowed. His hands went to Kao Ton's golden hips, he held her to him, he pushed and pushed and sobbed in the spilling of his fluids.

Somebody knocked on the door again.

Chapter Six

Cesare Iannotto jerked out of Kao Ton who collapsed on her belly, panting in the aftermath of her pleasures. I lay there, exhausted myself.

"Yeah, yeah. I'm coming," the button muttered.

He staggered to the door. I watched him through half closed eyes. He was weak now, all right. If I'd had the strength I could have run to him, knocked him unconscious with a judo blow and dropped on him with the pillow.

I just lay there and thought about it, while he opened the door. A hardfaced Chinese man was in the doorway, saying something in broken English. I listened with all my might.

"You got go now. Not safe, stay more."

"I know, I know. The train to Soochow. Right on, mac. Just lemme get my clothes on."

The hardfaced man stepped into the room. His

cold black eyes touched Kao Ton and me, and I tensed. Danger threatened us from those eyes. As soon as Scarface was gone, this man meant to kill us.

And why not? We were concubines, worth not very much even in the old days because we were females, worth not even that much today. When there were so many Chinese in the world, who could care if two girls got killed? I lay there and thought.

The tables had turned on me. I'd planned to tire the Mafia muscleman, instead I was the one lying here without the energy to lift a little finger.

Kao Ton was sleeping, her cheek pillowed on one of my thighs. I'd get no help there. So I rested, with nothing better to do. I certainly wasn't going to jump to my feet and scream.

I watched Cesare Iannotto dress. I had no chance to kill him now. He would walk out of here safely and take that train to Soochow. And I would be dead and buried long before he got there.

He went out into the hall. The hardfaced Chinese drew a long, slim knife from inside his jacket and came toward the bed. I tensed. I waited until he was an inch from the edge of the mattress and starting to bend over Kao Ton, knife upraised to plunge into her unprotected back.

My legs came up. My feet shot forward.

I caught his chest with one foot, the side of his jaw with the other. He let out a surprised squawk—he must have thought we were both sleeping—and reeled back, barely maintaining his balance.

I came off that bed like a bullet.

Naked I leaped for him. I knew damn well he would think me easy prey and bring up that knife to bury it in my belly. He didn't say a word, neither did I. He must be thinking me a pretty stupid female to lunge for that length of glittering steel in his hand, but at the same time he would be happy that I was making it so easy for him.

Inches from him his knifehand, I slid to a halt, digging in my heels. He had already started his move, the blade was coming for my belly.

Both my hands darted out, caught his wrist. I pivoted on a foot. My hip rammed into him just as I drew that knifearm across my shoulder. I heaved upward.

The Chinese went off his feet into the air.

I let go of him, jumped. As he came down, so did I. He landed on the floor, I landed on him, with both my heels sunk into his solar plexus. The air went out of his lungs and he writhed there, unable to utter a sound.

My hands went to his knife hand. I tore the blade free.

I drove that blade at his throat.

Just as the point sank into his flesh, his wildly rolling eyes settled on me. I saw an abysmal terror in those eyes, he knew he was a dead man, my face was merciless. Of course, I didn't dare let him live to howl the house down around us, his death was written on the looms of Tchi Nui and I was the one to carry it out.

I withdrew the knife after I was sure he was dead.

I cleansed it on his clothes, then tossed it toward my cheong-sam. That knife might come in handy again, I felt. Then I crossed to the bed, shook Kao Ton.

"We've got to get out of here," I told her opening eyes.

"Mmmmm, not yet. It's so nice to lie here, so warm."

My hands shook her again. "Look, Kao Ton."

She looked, and only my hand clapped over her lips kept her from screeching. Above my fingers, her lovely black eyes swung toward me, asked a question. I bent to whisper in her golden ear, in the best Chinese I could muster.

"Yes, yes. I had to kill him. He was all set to stab you in the back while you were sleeping."

I let my hand fall from her lips. She whispered, "What are we going to do? They will kill us, they don't want anybody to know about the man we were with, they are afraid we'll talk."

"Get dressed. We've got to get out of here."

She shook her head. "There is no way."

Kao Ton slid off the bed, the lamplight gleaming on her soft golden skin, her high breasts and flat belly. She walked gracefully to her clothes, lifted the cheong-sam above her long black hair. She slid into it with a twist of her torso and hips. As that garment fell about her nudity, I gave a little sigh.

"We'll leave the room and tiptoe down the hall. We must find some way of getting across the city."

"What about that doorman? He'll give the alarm."

I lifted the knife, showed it to her. Her eyes got big. "We'll just walk toward him, if he gives us any trouble he gets this." I made a motion with the knife and Kao Ton shivered.

I stepped over the dead man on the way to the door. I turned the knob, peered out into the hall. Nobody there. I motioned to Kao Ton and we ran as lightly as we could until we came to the wooden staircase. The boards had not creaked on the way up, so there was no reason to suspect they would do so on our way down. They didn't.

We ran across the dining room.

As we came into the lower hall, we saw the husky doorman sitting on his stool. He turned as we came toward him, Kao Ton in the lead, hands clasped and head bent a little.

"We have been dismissed," she told him.

He stared at her supiciously. "Lem Ho didn't say anything to me about it. All the girls stay here."

Kao Ton murmured, "We are not regular girls, we are only substitutes."

"What difference does that make?"

He turned to reach for a bell-pull. I stepped past

Kao Ton and drove the blade at his unprotected throat. He never suspected a thing. The steel went out of sight inside him, his body folded up, toppling lifeless from the stool. He thumped as he hit the floor, but by that time Kao Ton had the front door open and we ran out into the moonlit night.

We never looked back.

After a time, as we ran, I realized I was carrying a bloody knife that might leave a trail behind us. I stepped to one side, ran it into some earth inside a clay pot holding flowers, wiped the dirt off with my fingers, and sped after the Chinese girl.

There were no taxis in sight, we had to walk.

Fortunately, there is no street crime in Red China. Or if there is, nobody ever hears about it and we didn't see any signs of it. We walked and walked all through that seemingly endless night, until dawn was in the eastern sky and the day was all around us.

"The Kialing House is closer than your place, honey," I told her. "You'll stay with me."

She didn't fight me.

We crept into the hotel when everybody else was waking up. We got up to my room, threw ourselves on the bed fully clothed. We were beat.

Sometime during the day, Derek Guyfford came in and tried to wake us. I shooed him off, telling him we'd have dinner with him. Kao Ton was snoring lightly at the time, we whispered so as not to wake her. I clued him in about what had happened, that

Cesare Iannotto was still alive and I had a job yet to do.

"But right now, I couldn't care less about my job. I need shut-eye, Derek, so do be a nice boy and run away."

Twilight was in the air when we woke, fully refreshed.

The first thing we did was to step under a hot shower with a cake of soap in our hands and wash away the yellow dye from my skin. Kao Ton made a special froth of oils and soap she knew about, and removed the dye from my head hair and my mons veneris.

I was back to being redheaded Cherry Delight.

Kao Ton was much of a size with me so I loaned her one of my spare evening gowns, and wore the Marc Bohan. Derek was downstairs with Wing Dock; he had ordered a meal for us at the Kialing House, so we trooped in together.

Wing Dock was very pleased at what had taken place. How he learned about it, he would not say, but I knew damn well he had spies in the Golden Cloud House. Once he leaned across the table, as the waiter was preparing to serve us meat slice soup with a special sauce, and murmured, "You did very well, last evening. Everyone is most pleased."

He waited until the water was gone before he added, "The two men whom you sent to join their ancestors were very bad men, long hidden from us.

We are most grateful."

"You can show your gratitude by getting Derek and me to Soochow."

He nodded, smiling. "It is arranged. Just relax, Miss Delight. Enjoy the meal."

I certainly enjoyed it, all right. It was something special, as Kao Ton whispered to me on our way to the ladies room. Only visiting dignitaries whom the Red Chinese wanted to impress, were feasted in such a manner, on chicken walnut, on Pekingese sweet and sour pork, on kidneys with water chestnuts a la Cantonese and on Pineapple Duckling. No kidding, you got all those courses. You only ate a little of each, natch. There was the inevitable rice, but it tasted good with all the condiments on it.

I said, when I was fully stuffed, "Now let's get down to business. My victims have fled to Soochow, we have to go after them. Ought we to fly, Wing Dock?"

He considered this, head tilted. "It will give your Derek Guyfford more time to make his snapshots, if you do. And this is why he is in China."

I nodded, glancing at Derek who sat there with his face hanging out, perfectly motionless. He was letting me carry the ball. But when I told Wing Dock we would fly from Chungking to Soochow, Derek got an approving glint in his eyes.

The plane would leave tomorrow at noon, Wing Dock said. It would take us about five or six hours to get there, depending on the tail winds. It would beat the train by several days.

"Giving you and Derek Guyfford a chance to do your picture taking," smiled Wing Dock.

"Why didn't the Mafia boys fly?" I wondered.

Wing Dock shrugged. "Probably it will take time for these tong members you say exist in our society to get together. They will live in remote places, some of them. They may not be able to make it sooner."

We chatted a little more, Wing Dock promised to make all the arrangements, to have a taxi waiting for us to carry us and our luggage to the airport. In the meantime, he would see Kao Ton to her home.

Kao Ton and I embraced. I told her I liked her very much, that some day maybe I would be able to get a visa into China on my own, on a pleasure trip. Then we could go shopping together, ogle the sights, do all the things two girls do together.

I waved to her as she walked out into the night with Wing Dock. Derek took me by the arm, led me toward the elevator.

"I want to have a little talk, ducks," he murmured. "It'll be safest in your room. However, I must get my tape recorder to play a little music, a little chatter."

When I raised my eyebrows, he chuckled. "Surprised at you, ducks. You must know about bugs, eh? Don't trust these smiling Chinese. Not at all. Wouldn't surprise me in the least if both our rooms are being listened into."

"And you want to rap about something you don't want anybody to hear about except us two." His arm squeeze told me I was right.

We got his recorder, he turned it on as soon as we entered my room. He said quite loudly, so anyone listening in could hear him, "Ah, that's better, pet. A little soft music, a little light patter to keep us company."

Then in a soft voice, he muttered, "Want to talk about that treasure I'm after, ducks. And I most certainly don't want the Red Chinese government to learn of it."

I sprawled myself out on a sofa. Derek pulled a chair closer. He put the tape recorder and player on a table, turned the volume high.

He said, "There are some caves close by Soochow which pirates used to use, centuries ago. Some of them have been outfitted very nicely. It's in one of those caves that the treasure the tong boys took from the Imperial Palace during the Boxer rebellion is stored."

"And we intend to rob it."

"Only some of it, pet. The choicest items."

"Such as?"

"The diamonds known as the Tears of Kouan-in, who was the goddess of mercy in the old Chinese pantheon. They are five in number, all reputed to be the most perfect blue white stones in existence, each over five hundred carats. One alone would cost a million dollars. Maybe even more.'

"Then there's the emeralds which are known as the Eggs of Chi Nong, the god who taught men to cook. Each is as large as a walnut, as perfectly shaped. Not to mention other jewels, equally perfect, and that pearl which is the *ch'u-nu*, the untouched virgin, because it has no flaw."

He grinned, "For half of these, for even one, I would risk my life. No man knows the extent of the fortune of the emperors and empresses of China. The records were destroyed. By the Boxers? By the looters from the western nations? Who knows? They are gone, and only legend lingers. And legend says the tong men have them put away in one of those caves."

"First we have to catch up to my Mafia buttons," I said determinedly, fighting back the vision of just one of the Tears of Kouan-in on a pendant about my neck when I went out on a dinner date with Mark Condon.

"Of course, ducks. That's understood. And we have to take my pictures. But fall asleep tonight and think of those jewels just waiting to be picked up and carried back to civilization by us. Eh?"

He leaned to pat my knee, picked up his tape recorder and player and carried it to the door. Just before he stepped out into the hall, he shut it off.

Me, I dreamed I was lost on a desert of diamonds

and had absolutely no water at all until I crushed the diamonds, one by one, and got a single drop of water from each. When my thirst was finally quenched, the diamonds were all gone. I sat on those desert sands and wailed.

My tears turned into emeralds. I started picking them up, staggering around here and there, but I could only carry so many. Then a wind began blowing and carried me and the emeralds up high into the sky. I began to fall

My body hit the floor. I had fallen out of bed. It was nine o'clock.

I gave a great big sigh and started getting dressed. I had my bags packed and was ready to go down and have breakfast when Derek knocked.

"We eat, then a taxi will take us to the airport," he told me. "Sometime tonight, we'll be sleeping in Soochow."

Inside two hours, we were in the air.

The flight to Soochow was uneventful. As are most flights once you are in the air, it was vaguely boring. The engines droned, the plane flew on, the land was below you, looking oddly like a model of what the Earth should look like.

We descended through a squalling rain onto Soochow airfield. It was a small place compared to Kennedy International or O'Hare or Los Angeles Airport, but it was neat and clean. We came down the ramp to find a taxi waiting us and were swept away to a private home overlooking Lake Tai. The house was spacious, built in several layers, modernistic in tone with none of the traditional Chinese style about it. Several of the flat roofs were sunbathing decks, or decks where orange trees were growing in big, earthenware pots.

Derek was very grim about his photography, now. I think he felt he'd given me enough time to get my Mafia button and that I'd failed on the job, so these were his innings coming up. I had no objection. I felt pretty downhearted about the whole bit.

So we walked the streets, taking the same sort of pictures of food shops filled with edibles for the inhabitants of this city, we saw those inhabitants emerge to sweep up fallen treebranches and such after a rainstorm, we snapped them coming and going.

After three days, Derek asked our guide if we could take snapshots of the countryside in its sweep toward the East China Sea. The guide, a middle-aged Chinaman whose moon face was expressionless for most of the time, showed alarm and stated that he would have to ask his superiors.

"The coast is lovely at this time of year," the Englishman went on. "I think you'd be doing your land an injustice not to include it along with shots of the cities and the hardworking people going their best to live up to the sayings of the great Mao Tse-tung. Remember, the western world doesn't realize how lovely some of your trees are, nor have they ever seen the solemnity of your wonderful coastline."

He laid it on with a shovel, but the guide blinked and looked pleased. I felt certain every word Derek said would be repeated to those superiors.

We spent another day photographing the same old things.

Then we got the word. We were to have a Shanghai sedan at our disposal, Derek would drive, but would go only where the guide told him.

I ordered a big basket lunch from the chef at the private house where we were staying. I didn't know how long we were going to be, so I felt it best to be prepared. Derek laughed when he saw the two wicker baskets crammed with cold chickens and fruit, sandwiches and thermos bottles.

"Not afraid of starving to death, are you, pet?" he asked.

"You never know," I muttered morosely.

The day was lovely as we started out. We took a few snaps of Lake Tai, then headed eastward toward the coast. We moved through a countryside where the eternal rice paddies lay wet and lush in the hot sun. North of us were the Great China Plains, where potatoes were raised and huge wheat fields rippled in the winds off the rivers that lay like silver ribbons across the land.

We pulled over to the side of the road. Derek would take some pictures, then we would be on our way again. We drove and stopped, drove and stopped, until I started to doze from the monotony of it all.

A little past noon we were at the coast.

"Time to eat," said Derek.

We picked a sweeping meadowland that over-looked the estuary of the Yangtze where it sweeps outward into the East China Sea. Across the bay lay a big island, but it was not in this that Derek was inter-ested. He wandered here and there with his cameras, while I set out our food.

When he returned to us to munch on cold chicken and a sandwich, he had a satisfied look on his face. He lifted a thermos of green tea, turned away, and poured a cup for our guide who was sit-ting there, stuffed to completion.

"A toast to Mao Tse-tung," Derek said.

The guide beamed. Derek poured tea for himself and for me. We raised our glasses, toasted the Chi-nese leader, and drank the tea. The Englishman sat quietly, as though waiting patiently. After about five minutes, our guide toppled over and lay motionless.

I turned wide eyes toward Derek. "You haven't killed him?"

"Hardly, ducks. I gave him a couple of sleeping pills. Now on your feet—and bring that compact camera I gave you."

We beat feet across the grass to the rocky head-land that brooded out over the sea. Derek began to unwind a thin rope from his lean middle.

"Here's where we go treasure hunting, love. Here, let me put this about that pretty waist of yours."

He tied the rope to me, then let it out slowly.

I went over the edge of the cliff, dropped down it and began lowering myself with the big Englishman playing out the strand. I told myself I was an utter nitwit to be playing at games with Derek Guyfford when there was N.Y.M.P.H.O. work to be done, but here in China, unless you had a guide to go with you, you went only where the guide was allowed to take you.

After I'd gone down about two dozen feet, I came to an opening in the wall.

"There's a cave here, Derek," I called up.

"Slide in, pet. And loosen the rope."

I moved into cold gloom and damp stone floor and walls. From the sea, this little entryway would appear to be no more than a dark shadow. You had to get up real close to learn that it was not part of the blackish veins that ran through this grey rock, here and there. I crouched in the gloom and waited.

Derek came sliding down, joined me. He had left his cameras behind, but he carried a big flashlight. He played its rays ahead of us and I saw a winding tunnel formed out of solid rock with a slippery, jagged floor.

"Follow me, ducks," he muttered.

His light was a brightness that showed us wet

walls and a low ceiling where Derek and I both had to duck down at times to avoid cracking our skulls. The further into the cave we went, the wider the tunnel became, the smoother the floor.

"The way I heard the story is," said the Englishman, "that this was used by junk pirates, centuries ago, and was found by the tong men when they needed a secret place to meet. Nobody but nobody outside the tong boys know of this."

"How did you learn?"

"Wing Dock. He can't come here, so he sent me. I'm to bring out some jewels for him. We made a deal, you see. Here I was with a visa, I could go about anywhere I wanted in Red China—which he couldn't—and so he offered to make me his partner.

"When the tongs took over this place, they used it to store their loot, their ill-gotten treasures from the Peking palace at the time of the Boxer rebellion. Be prepared to scream in delight at what you see, ducks —but don't."

We followed that tunnel for close to half a mile before we came to a vast, black cavern. Then Derek lifted his beam.

I clapped a hand to my mouth.

The first thing I saw was an open teakwood box, half filled with diamonds spilling over onto what must have been a priceless Turkish carpet, at one time. Now it was moldy, rotted, but it served to show those diamonds, as that torch beam hit them, like a blue velvet pad in Tiffany's. All the colors of the rainbow sparkled and scintillated there, in a very river of gems.

I started to push Derek to one side.

"Easy, pet. That's the cheap stuff you're looking at. There's more and better to come. Just follow old Derek."

He tried to speak naturally, but I caught the throb of wild excitement in his voice. And I didn't blame him. We were staring our eyes out at a cave filled with what must have been several billions of dollars, always assuming you could find a market for this stuff.

Because as he swept the beam here and there, I made out silk paintings, rare statues and vases that took the breath away with their beauty. Here were hidden away the works of those masters of the brush that traditional China revered for their artistic creations. This was a repository for the paintings of the almost legendary Chin K'o and Kuan Hsui, of Mu Chi and Liang K'ai. I saw statues of the mythical queen of the West, Hsi Wang Mu, done in solid gold, there were carvings in jade of that greatest satyrist of all the Chinese, Shou Lou, of whom it is said that he lived so long because he had coupled with so many women in his lifetime.

Jade was everywhere, as if it were no more than stoneware. Ginger jars and cricket cages in solid gold, in silver and rimmed with precious stones, breathtaking porcelains, here was stored the art productions of the ages. I saw in a dim corner the yak standards and horsetail banners of Genghis Khan, I saw the robes of state of countless emperors of the Ming and Sung and Tang dynasties. Everywhere my eyes went, riches were piled upon riches.

And the jewels!

I ran to one table where five small boxes stood. I threw back the lids and stared at emeralds and rubies, sapphires and pearls tossed helterskelter together as though by a careless hand. My fingers dipped into them, I lifted them as a child might grains of sand and let them run through my fingers,

"Couldn't I slip a few into my pockets?" I begged.

"That's just chickenfeed, ducks."

It might have been chickenfeed to Derek Guyfford but I could see a diamond and emerald necklace, a diamond and ruby bracelet, diamond earrings and God knows how many priceless rings, all for me, if I could ever get some of these gems out of here and into a Fifth Avenue store to have them set.

I almost cried when he dragged me away.

But Derek knew what he was doing. His flashlight went this way and that as we went deeper and deeper into the recesses of this vast cavern that seemed to stretch out endlessly under the land. At one time, ages ago, the ocean had probably pounded in here, wearing away the stone to form it. Now we passed between chests of golden coins, scattered ropes of pearls, piles of antique lacquered armor and helmets.

At last we stood before a great chest of carved teak.

"You got a hairpin on you, ducks? We have to open that lock."

I grinned. As a member of the N.Y.M.P.H.O. gang, I always carry a cleverly disguised picklock on my key chain. I knelt down, snapped open the picklock and went to work. In a matter of seconds, the chest door swung open.

There were a number of small porcelain coffers inside. Derek said, "Lift them out, pet—but be careful."

One by one I raised them to the top of the chest. I let Derek open them, they were his babies to show off, but I crowded close so as not to miss a thing. The lids went back, one after the other. I bit my lower lip to stifle my cry of surprise.

I was staring down at gigantic diamonds, massive emeralds, huge rubies. The diamonds were flawless, bluish white, reflecting all the colors known to man. The emeralds were green flames trapped in three dimensions. And the rubies were the color of blood, heavy and perfectly cut.

"Oh my God," I whimpered.

"The Tears of Kouan-in," he whispered, pointing.

There were five diamonds in all, seemingly all perfectly matched. They were immense, they were about the size of ping pong balls. 1 lifted two in my hands, cradled them on my palms. Just one of these would have made me independently rich for life.

Derek breathed, "The Eggs of Chi Nong."

I placed the diamonds back into their porcelain boxes, lifted out the three emeralds. They seemed to throb in my grip, and where the light caught their verdant depths a tiny flame flickered.

"And the *ch'u-nu*, the untouched virgin."

The *ch'u-nu* was a giant pearl, shaped like a globe. It was round and smooth, its lustre was dazzling. One could only stare at its size and beauty in a kind of bemused state. There have been legends of pearls as large as this, as perfect, but I'd always before believed them to be old wives tales.

I wanted to tell Derek Guyfford to stuff our pockets with them, to forget about the Mafia buttons, to get the hell out of here with these things and live the rest of our lives in utter leisure.

A nagging thought touched my mind.

I had a duty to perform not only for N.Y.M.P.H.O. but for the memory of Bill Tomkins as well. I sighed, lifted the Untouched Virgin to my cheeks and caressed it.

"Put it back, pet," he said.

"Put it back? Aren't you going to take it along? And these other jewels? You surely don't intend leaving these things here?"

"Matter of fact, I do."

"But why? It would be so easy. . . ."

"Ducks, the border guards are going to search our luggage, they'd find these things and take 'em away with them. We'll finish our job, come back here with a boat some dark night, and get what we want."

"And get shot by a coast patrol boat," I commented bitterly.

"Aren't they worth a little risk?"

I shrugged. Maybe he was right. He knew the Red Chinese customs far better than I. I put the *ch'u-nu* back into its box, closed the lid regretfully.

That was when the cavern blazed with lights.

Chapter Seven

I stood frozen with disbelief.

There could be no such lights in this place! It was a dark sea cave. Except for the flashlight in Derek's hand, there was no illumination!

I whirled. Derek had already turned, staring.

Three Chinamen in plain linen suits were facing us at a distance, revolvers in their hands. The revolvers were aimed at us. Slightly behind them were other Chinese, and two men I knew for Mafia buttons. Above their heads, a string of electric lights blazed brightly.

Of course, I recognized Scarface, though by the way he was staring at me I'm sure he didn't realize I was the singsong girl he'd played sex games with back in Chunking. Beside him was a heavy set man who just had to be the Big Tommy that Cesare Iannotto had mentioned.

"You will please come forward, hands up."

Derek and I obeyed promptly. You don't argue with men who have their guns trained on your bellybuttons. Other Chinese sprang forward, grabbed Derek, swung him around and tied ropes to his wrists. Me they treated only slightly less roughly, also binding my wrists. From somewhere deep in the cave a generator hummed.

A gun gestured Big Tommy forward.

"What are you two doing here?" he asked.

"Sightseeing," I murmured, when Derek was silent. "You see, we're in Red China on a visa that permits my companion to take pictures. All this is being done on the authority of the great Mao Tse-tung."

The faces of the Chinese were serious, grave. They knew better than any of us what it might mean to interfere with guests of the state.

"Then how cone you're in here?" asked Scarface.

"We were hunting for flowers, I wanted to make a bouquet. I saw the little cave entrance, we came down here." I asked innocently, "Why? Have we done anything wrong?"

One of the tong men had been listening closely to us as we spoke. I was sure he understood English; after all, neither Scarface nor Big Tommy savvied Chinese, so somebody had to be able to interpret. Maybe he didn't want Derek and me to know that he understood our talk.

He saw me eyeballing him, he must have realized I'd guessed he spoke English. He gave me a grim smile, said, "All this may be as you have said. I have heard rumors that an Englishman and his assistant were in Soochow, taking pictures. But this is far from Soochow."

"We wanted snapshots of your lovely countryside. We left our guide sleeping and took a walk."

"I do not believe you. I must know how you knew about the caves of the treasures of the Imperial Dowager. And so. . . ."

He gestured, spoke in Chinese.

Men ran in all directions. They came back carrying objects that I could tell with one quick look were torture instruments. I started shaking in my shoes.

Chinese executioners in the past have been renowned for the variety and imaginativeness of the tortures to which they put the poor slobs whom their rulers wanted tortured. There is the water torture, which is pretty famous, in which a man is tied down so he cannot move his head and a drop of water falls on his forehead steadily and without stopping. Maybe it doesn't sound like much but it drives men mad.

Then there is the death of the thousand caresses, in which concubines caress a man in relays, never permitting him to orgasm, until his heart bursts. There was the 'frame of the lowering eyebrow', 'the monkey grasping the peach', and 'smoking in a tube'. Flowery names for the giving of incredible pain.

I wondered what our fate was to be.

Somebody threw a rope over a jutting rock tongue that was part of the cave wall. The other end of the rope was looped to Derek's tied hands. Three tong members pulled on the rope end while Derek's arms were bent far behind him and his body was lifted upward until he was just touching the stone floor with his toes. His suffering was written in his face.

Then they came for me.

I considered fighting; better to die than suffer the agonies in store for me, but with my hands tied behind my back, I couldn't put up too much of a battle, save with my feet. So I bided my time.

Cesare Iannotto and Big Tommy were grinning, relishing what was going to happen. Two tong members came for me, yanked and jerked at my clothes until they were in shreds. Then they used sharp knives to cut them away completely, leaving me stark naked.

The Chinese boys and the Mafia buttons hissed in their throats at sight of my pink nudity. With my wrists still bound I was brought forward toward a table that had leather straps hanging from it. Two of them were fastened to wooden arms that rose up into the air at one end. I wondered what their purpose was. I soon found out.

I was thrown down on my back, my knees were slipped into the straps, the straps were tightened so that my thighs were spread wide apart. At the same time my hands were freed and my wrists were imprisoned in straps on either side of the table. I lay spread-eagled there, utterly helpless. Sweatbeads came out on my forehead.

One of the tong men stepped close. He had a bamboo stick in his hand about three feet long and two inches wide, it looked very springy.

"Is different version of the bastinado," said the Chinese who could understand and speak English. "Mostly man gets beaten on buttocks with bamboo stick. Light blows, not hard. Seems like not much. Pretty soon flesh turns blue, man screams and fights to get away. Is hurt lots."

The guy began whipping my genital lips. It didn't hurt, at first. Then the pain became so excruciating, I screamed. I went on screaming, my hips lifting, trying to get away from that bamboo sliver, but I couldn't. I was sure I was bleeding all over the place, there in my crotch. To my fevered imagination, my pussylips were being pounded to bloody pulp.

"You'd better talk," said Scarface, licking his lips.

It was getting to him, he bulged his pants, as did Big Tommy and even the *bow how doy* boys. There was sweat on their faces, too, but it wasn't the sweat of pain. Faintly, I could hear Derek Guyfford moaning.

"Why don't we sample some of that before you turn it into a bloody froth?" asked Scarface hoarsely.

"I wouldn't mind getting my rocks off in that, either," growled Big Tommy.

The Chinese chattered among themselves, laughing lewdly. I guess they figured they might as well get in on the fun, there was nobody around to stop them and—what the hell!—nobody ever got enough sex in Red China these days.

They stripped down, the whole lot of them.

One of the Chinese put his clothes on the table so that they lay across my right arm. Then they lined up.

Big Tommy came at me first. He was a hairy guy, very muscular but starting to turn to fat. His clothes had been close to bursting at their seams. He was a big man, essentially a sadist, I think, because he sure had enjoyed seeing my poor pussylips getting bastinadoed.

He took his time, enjoying the fact that I was unexcited, that I was dry down there and that it hurt like hell as he went into my lacerated parts. I cursed him monotonously, my head sliding back and forth in deference to the agony in my flesh, while he grinned down at me and sawed away.

After a time he withdrew, spent, and a Chinaman took his place. There were nine Chinamen in all, and the Mafia buttons made eleven men I was made to service, and they all came back for seconds. Each one hurt worse than the last. I was sobbing and weeping, freaked out, long before they were done with me.

Now I enjoy sex as well as, or maybe even better than the next guy or gal, but I don't believe in forcible rape. Still, there wasn't anything I could do about it. I lay there and suffered, and felt I was going mad. During all this time, my hands were opening and closing. I found—when my mind returned to sanity from moment to moment—that I was clutching the discarded garments of that tong boy who'd been in such a hurry to undress he'd thrown his clothes on me.

I was clutching something else, too, occasionally.

My crisping fingers told me it was the handle of a hammer. But this didn't make any sense. What would a tong hatchet man be doing with a hammer? Then it dawned on me. It wasn't a hammer but some sort of ceremonial axe.

My hand tightened on it.

I held onto that handle for dear life, all through the rest of my raping. The Mafia buttons and the Chinese sweated and strained, grunted and swore as they pounded their organs in my poor private parts. Eventually, they were done.

One of the naked Chinese said something which delighted all the others. The interpreter translated, "We are going to have some more fun with this one. We are about to perform the *'ling chez'* on her. 'The death of a thousand cuts'. We have a garment here that was made many, many years ago for just such a purpose."

A man came forward carrying what appeared to be a decrepit shirt of mesh mail. I say decrepit because there were slits all over it. It had thongs of leather to lace it up the back. There were sleeves to the thing, even mailed legs.

"We must put her in it," said a tong man.

Somebody came and loosened my straps. They let my feet down first, then they came to my wrists. One after the other, they freed them. I lay there without moving, trying to pull myself together. I didn't know what the 'ling chez' torture was, but it didn't sound very nice.

I am sure the tong boys didn't expect me to put up a fight. After all, I was a lone, naked female in here with them. What could I do?

My hand was still wrapped about that hatchet handle, however.

Sure, sure. My body had been tortured and raped, but when one faces death by the 'thousand cuts'—whatever that was—one summons up the strength from somewhere to fight back.

So as both my hands and legs came free, I gripped that hatchet and swung it at the nearest yellow face. I didn't even bother taking it out of the clothes that held it. The owner of the blade must have kept the edge honed to the sharpness of a razor, because it went right into the face of the surprised man bending over my right wrist, fingers extended to grasp it.

He died on his feet.

I jerked the axe free and swung around on my rump to deliver a blow at the man to my right. The edge caught him across the neck and sheared through it. Then I was off that table and running—straight for one of the men I knew had a revolver.

They were frozen motionless with amazement.

I hurt like hell between my thighs but I would have hurt far worse all over me if I hadn't come bounding like a crazy Amazon straight for my enemies. I managed to shake the bloody hatchet free of the clothes that had been around it, and slammed the edge at another face.

The blade went deep. I let go of the handle, dove for the clothes this character had dropped on the floor. My fingers went around a gunbutt.

I lifted the revolver, fired.

A man dropped.

The others screeched and scattered, yelling in Chinese to each other. I noted that Scarface and Big Tommy were among the first ones to disappear. Me, I leaped for cover, too—behind one of the chests that held some of the Imperial treasures.

Silence lay like a curtain over the cave.

Every last one of us was stark naked except for Derek Guyfford. He hung from his arms that were held up behind him, his toes barely touching the floor. I could see him out of the corner of my eyes, but I couldn't get to him without exposing myself.

Then it dawned on me.

All the clothes with the revolvers and hatchets in them were on the stone floor around my torture table. I was the only one who had a gun. I checked the cylinder. There were four bullets left.

I walked out onto the open space where the clothes had been dropped. What the hell! Nobody could shoot me, the guns were there in the discarded clothes. I bent over to yank out another revolver.

"Cherry—watch yourself!" Derek cried.

I dropped to my knees, turned. One of the Chinamen was running for me, a long lance in his hand. Probably a Mongol chieftain had carried that thing into battle when Genghis Khan had been known as the Scourge of the Earth. Its still sharp point was aimed right for my face.

My finger triggered the gun even as I dove to one side. The lance passed over me, its head almost getting my bare arm. The man carrying it was dead before he fell into me, bowling me over.

As I fell, a Chinese screamed.

They came from all directions, four of them. They were naked, but I was only one. A man left his feet, dove for me. I'd lost the guns in my hands when that dead body catapulted into me. So I lifted a bare leg, grabbed one of his arms and heaved him over me.

He went like a stone flung from a catapult and cannoned into one of his fellows. They went down in a heap.

Two others fell on top of me. I was like a raging wildcat, I guess, half mad with determination not to be tortured any more. I opened my mouth, sank my teeth into flesh—it was a man's belly—and bit as deep as I could. A scream told me I was hurting whoever had fallen on me.

I dug my long red fingernails into a face, ran them downward. I drew blood, I could feel it oozing around my fingertips. Somebody else screamed.

Then I was squirming out from under those men, diving for my dropped guns. One was fully loaded, the other had only three bullets. I didn't know which was which, so I grabbed them both, I fired at the four remaining Chinamen, dropping them one by one until none were left alive.

As I did so, a Mafia button yelled; "Drop it, baby!"

I turned my head.

Scarface was standing there with his cannon aimed right at me. If I made a move, his finger would tighten on the trigger and I would be one dead girl. I had been so close to success! If only I'd remembered that Scarface and Big Tommy were here in the cave! I believed them to be unarmed, after all, they were as naked as jaybirds.

Maybe Scarface read my thoughts. He said, "We tossed our clothes in the shadows, lady. It was easy for us to grab our guns while you were takin' care of them Chinks."

His eyes ran around the cavern. "Ya know, maybe we owe ya a good turn for that. This is quite a place, ain't it?"

Big Tommy came into view, pulling up his pants. Above his belt he was hairy, fat, monstrous. He growled, "You talk too much, Cesare."

"Ah, what harm Tommasso? The dame's as good as dead."

The big man walked in among the chests of jewels, of golden coins. He ran his pudgy fingertips over them almost lovingly. "Cesare, I'm getting an idea. These tong characters are all dead. We got their agreements about the trade, what say we cut ourselves in on some of this stuff, take back a few souvenirs of our visit?"

"I don't know, Tommy. Other tong men were to meet us here. They haven't come yet, but I wouldn't want them to catch us . . ."

Greed warred with caution inside Cesare Iannotto. His eyes ran from me to the jewels, back to me again. His gun did not waver, otherwise I might have risked a flying leap at him. His tongue came out to lick around his lips.

"You think we could get away with it?"

"Hell, them Chinks are dead. Who's to stop us?"

"Nobody, I guess. You, girl—toss them guns over here!"

I almost took the chance. All I would have to is turn the barrels his way and start pulling trigger. Yeah, man. By the time I swivelled them half around, his bullets would be in my gut, It was a bummer.

I slid the guns across the floor to him.

Cesare grinned. I was unarmed, now. Naked. He wriggled the gun. "Over there with your friend. Tommy, give me a hand. Then we can take our time without having to worry about either of them."

They came toward me, they caught my hands and fastened them the same way Derek's hands were tied, behind my back. They attached a longer rope, drew it up over the same rock tongue from which Derek was hung and hoisted me up. They didn't raise me quite so far as the tong boys had lifted the Englishman, they had no desire to hurt me. They just wanted me out of the way.

So I said, "Why not lower him a little? He's up on his toes, his arms must feel like they're falling off."

Tommasso nodded. So they let him rest his feet, with his arms only halfway up. It was a lot easier on him and Derek muttered his thanks. Then they walked away and left us.

We watched them roam the cave, bending over this chest and then another. They picked out hand-fulls of diamonds and emeralds, none of which matched the Tears of Kouan-in nor the Eggs of Chi Nong, but they were pretty damn valuable, just the same. I'd say at a guess they filled their clothes with about five million dollars in jewels.

They ignored the gold. Hell, I couldn't blame them, gold prices being what they were on the world market, these days.

They took their time, they were in no hurry.

Of course, while they were busy with the jewels, I was trying to work on the ropes that bound Derek and me. I got nowhere. Those tong characters and the Mafia buttons had tied damn tight knots. They wouldn't budge an inch. I'd have needed a pliers to loosen them. So we hung there and watched the bastards get rich.

Finally Scarface came sauntering over, a gun in his hand. He put the muzzle to my left breast and pushed. Not hard, just a little. Then he grinned at me.

"I ought to kill you, you know," he said conversationally. "That way, there won't be anybody left to tell what happened here. There'll just be a lot of dead people. And dead men don't talk, lady."

"If you don't kill us, we'll starve to death, or die of thirst," I told him.

His mean little eyes got bright. "Hey, that's right. What do you say, Tommy? We kill them or leave them here to die by themselves?"

"Nobody could hear them yell," muttered Tommasso

"It would take them longer. Hurt more, too."

"Kind of too bad to let a hole like that die."

"We can't take her with us."

I listened to their discussion of my fate with rage boiling inside me. The damn, murdering skunks! I wished I had my hands free, just for about five minutes.

Scarface took his gun away from my breast. He tucked it into his shoulder holster. He was grinning steadily all the time. Big Tommy was studying us with his little eyes sunk in fat cheeks. I think he was balancing whys and wherefors, he didn't talk as much as Cesare Iannotto; he was the boss, however. I tabbed him for a *caporegime*, or lieutenant in the Mafia family.

"Leave 'em," he said suddenly.

Scarface reached behind me, patted me on the buttocks. "So long, doll. You were fun for a time. Too bad it's all over."

He walked after Big Tommy who was strolling lazily toward the opposite end of the cave, where the rock tunnel led upward to the surface and to safety. They took their time, they even turned around and stared at the cave as if memorizing it. Scarface winked at me.

Then they were gone.

Derek and I hung in those ropes, not saying a word.

After a time he muttered, "Ducks, I almost wish they'd shot us."

"At least, we're still alive."

"We'll live for a few days. Then thirst will get us."

I moved about, thinking. I was a few feet from Derek by this time and I began to laugh. I laughed so hard I damn near peed. All the time Derek Guyfford was making soothing sounds. The poor guy thought I was going bonkers.

"My teeth," I said finally, when I could.

"What?"

"I've been telling myself I needed a pair of pliers to loosen those knots and all the time I had a pair on me, in my head. My teeth, dummy! Now turn around."

He showed me his back. I bent over, closed my pearly whites about one of the knot ropes and tugged. He braced himself, which he was able to do with his feet on the rock floor. I pulled and yanked, tore at those ropes with my teeth until my gums bled, and just when I thought I'd never get them loose, the knot gave.

After that, it was only a question of time.

Derek shook himself free of the ropes, undid mine.

He moved around the cave, testing his arms and legs. "It hurts a bit, pet, but nothing like it did. I thought my muscles were being torn. I'll be all right in a jiff."

I moved toward my clothes, picked them up and put them on.

"Derek, we're sitting in the catbird seat," I said suddenly.

"If you say so, pet. We're alive, and I've a feeling we're going to get out of this in one piece. Thanks to you."

"The Eggs of Chi Nong, the Tears of Kouan-in and the Untouched Virgin."

"What about them?"

"Not going to leave them here, are you?"

"I am, ducks. I don't dare try and take them out of Red China."

"They fit inside your cameras."

His eyes got big and round. "By God, they would! With a little cotton stuffed in to make sure they didn't rattle, by taking out the film in one and maybe two of the cameras, we might get away with it. They'll see cameras, they won't be thinking of jewels inside them."

We raced for the teakwood chest. I did my thing with the picklock and one by one, Derek and I lifted out the diamonds, the emeralds, the big pearl. We put them in our pockets. Then we covered the porcelain containers and put them back inside the cabinet. I closed and locked it.

Derek was grinning from ear to ear. Me too.

"Now if we can only fool our guide long enough for me to slip these into two cameras, we're just about home free," he commented.

His hand reached for mine. We walked for the tunnelway.

And we heard voices.

Chapter Eight

I stared at Derek in holy horror.

Those were Chinese voices. And blended with them were the voices of Scarface and Big Tommy. It seemed to me the Mafia men were pleading or begging, but since I couldn't distinguish their words, I wasn't sure.

"What'll we do?" I whispered.

Derek still had hold of my hand. He gave it a yank and I went off my feet as I turned in midair and came down running. He was sliding between the Mongol banners and the chests into the darkest corner of the big cavern.

Under his breath he muttered, "My informant told me there are all sorts of smaller caves adjoining this one. If we can get into them, maybe we can lose them."

We ran like hell, but quietly.

A small opening appeared like magic to our left. We dove for it. It was another cave, and we ran into it. From its edge, we could peer into the big cave, and now we saw the two Mafia buttons being pushed along in front of about ten Chinese.

"You not run, you wait," said a tong man.

"We wasn't runnin'," protested Scarface.

"Liar!" cried the Chinaman. "Look how your pockets bulge. And when we—"

They came fully into the cavern now. They saw the dead bodies scattered around. The words the Chinaman had been speaking snapped shut with an angry click of his teeth.

"*Siu fan ti!*"

"Dead! All dead! Our friends!"

"Now look," Big Tommy growled. "We had nothing to do with that. It was the girl who killed them."

"Girl? What girl?"

For the first time, Scarface and Big Tommy saw I was not in the ropes, that Derek Guyfford was not there, either. I was peeping around a corner of the cave wall, I could see their faces turn ashen.

"She was here!" Scarface almost screamed. "Her and the man. They were tied up in those ropes. She was naked. She killed them. She—"

A tong man backhanded the hysterical button.

"I see two ropes on the floor. No traces of a naked girl or a man. Explain to us please, how a naked girl could have killed nine tong *bow how doys!*"

He made a good attempt. But listening to him, even knowing that I had done the killing, I still found it incredible. And when I peeped from hard yellow face to hard yellow face, I could read the reaction of his listeners.

"Nine men, all killed by a naked girl," said his main tormentor.

"Yeah, yeah. It happened."

"Then where is she? Where is her companion?"

"How do I know? We just left them and walked out. They were tied up with ropes slung over that chunk of rock. They couldn't move. We left them to die of starvation or maybe of thirst before that."

A Chinaman smiled. "You were gone—how long? Ten minutes at most? In that time you ask us to believe a naked man and a naked girl escaped—even you admitted they could not move—and then disappeared into thin air."

"They're here. They're here. They got to be!"

"The man is mad."

"No," screamed Scarface, reading those hard faces around him. "No, no! You've got to believe me. A naked girl did kill those nine men. And then Tommy and I tied her up. I—I don't know what happened to her . . ."

The Chinamen moved, they grabbed the Mafia buttons, they sought to tie their arms behind their backs. The gangsters put up a good fight, they were battling for their lives. Scarface got his gun out but it was knocked from his hand and went skidding across the floor. Big Tommy took three of the *bow how doy* boys off their feet, he was so big and strong, but it didn't do him much good. One man yanked his gun from its holster and tossed it.

Then the others moved in, fists flying. They didn't use their hatchets, they wanted the buttons alive. The doomed men fought with the desperation of men who knew that death awaited them. Fists flew, here and there a tong member went down to lie without moving.

Yet in the end, Scarface gave way, his knees buckling, crying out as he was borne backward to crash against a chest. Hands held him down as other hands ripped away his clothing, leaving him naked.

And the other Mafia man, though he lasted longer for his strength was greater, eventually gave way to larger numbers. He went to a knee, a foot caught him across a temple, he toppled over and lay inert as he, too, was stripped.

Derek and I watched from our hiding place.

We saw two tong members bring forward that curiously decrepit coat of linked metal. They slid its legs and arms over those of Big Tommy, fitted the thing to his body. A rope was tossed to that same rock tongue from which Derek and I had been suspended, was drawn taut.

Big Tommy hung there helpless, his toes barely touching the stone floor. Now two Chinamen went behind him, drew tight the leather lacings at the back of the metal suit. They made it so tight that pieces of his flesh protruded between the spaces in the linked mail that had made me believe it was useless.

A tong *bow how doy* approached, a case of what appeared to be slim knives in his hands. He said softly, "It has been many years since anyone was killed in the *'ling chez'* manner. It is a very slow, very bloody death."

He came closer. I saw the flash of steel as he laid the sharp edge of a knife to a length of flesh protruding from the mail suit. Big Tommy watched him with bulging eyes, sobbing, trying to writhe aside. Since his toes barely touched the ground, he was unable to move.

The knife flashed, grew bloody as it cut.

Big Tommy screamed. A length of his flesh lay on the stone floor. The knife moved again and yet again. Slowly, the Chinaman was literally slicing the Mafia man to thumbits. Parts of his bleeding body lay on the floor. He was being slashed to nothingness, bit by bit.

I stared horrified, my stomach churning.

Just so might I have died!

Now the men behind Big Tommy were tightening the leather laces so that more of his flesh protruded between the spaces of the mail suit. From arms and thighs and belly, from chest and buttocks and back, that knife sliced the living flesh. The mail shirt was drenched in blood.

The Mafia man was moaning. He was not yet near death, the cuts only took a little of his flesh from him each time, but little by little, the pile of bleeding meat that had been a man was growing on the stone floor.

Scarface was white, ashen. His eyes bulged out, all whites. He was shaking steadily. Big Tommy was groaning, screaming to the pain, with the awareness that he was a dead man though he still lived. He was losing blood, and there must have been pounds of quivering meat on the floor at his feet.

I was going to be sick. Derek caught me, swung me away so that I couldn't see what was going on. I sobbed at the air, I drew it into my lungs. I felt so sorry for Big Tommy. A gangster he might be, cruel and merciless, and it was my job to see him dead.

Yet mine would have been a clean death-giving. A bullet in the heart, no more. The *bow how doys* were not content with that, Big Tommy had tried to cheat them, he had killed nine of their fellows—or so they believed—and so he had to die in as slow and painful a method as they knew.

A Chinaman said calmly, "Tales have been told that some men are cut into such small pieces, their meat is not recognizable as human, when the executioner is done. Just the hands and the feet remain."

Now a mailed mask that fitted over the head was

brought and Big Tommy really screamed, knowing what would happen. But before the knife went to work on his head, salt was sprinkled on his wounds, and lime, and rubbed in so that the agony must have been awful. He still lived, no vital part of him had been harmed.

This would take hours.

I buried my face against Derek Guyfford, felt his arms go about me as though to shelter me from the screams.

I don't know how long we stood this way, with my hands clamped over my ears and my shuddering weight leaning against the Englishman. But eventually even I noticed the cave was quiet, so I pushed away and looked again.

My horrified eyes went to a pile of bloody flesh that lay with two bare feet and what was left of an eyeless head. That had been a man, my mind told me. That had been Big Tommy.

Then I looked at Scarface. He had fainted when the tong men had come for him. I guess he expected to be laced up in that same mail suit, to have his own body sliced to ribbons.

The *bow how doys* had something else in mind for him.

One of them said, "There is a special form of bamboo shoot that grows a foot in one day. In the old days, men used to stake a man or a woman over a tiny shoot of that bamboo plant and keep it watered so that it grew right through the man or woman while he or she was still alive.

"Unfortunately, we don't have time for such niceties. You are to die more swiftly. Though perhaps— just as painfully. You see, what we are going to do to you is something different."

He clapped his hands and two tong men brought a fire-box and a long, thin flexible steel whip with wooden handle attached. The steel whip was pushed inside the firebox where coals had been ignited. Scarface, who was strung up by his wrists naked, could only stare and moan very softly.

When the steel whip was white-hot, a man lifted it from the firebox and took up his position behind Scarface. He struck hard, the heated steel sizzled when it touched the man; Cesare Iannotto screamed, head back, for the hot metal went into his flesh.

The flogger left it there a moment. The flesh bubbled over it in seconds. Then the flogger yanked it out. The pain must have been excruciating. The whip was pushed into the firebox, brought out white-hot. Again it lashed Scarface across his back, there was a wait, and the rod was pulled out.

It went on for hours.

Until the mindless thing that had been a muscleman for the Mafia lay hung limp and lifeless in the ropes that held him up. His entire body was a mass of torn, burned flesh, from knees to neck. He had screamed until his voice was no more than a croak, he had bitten away his lower lip in his agony.

Now he was dead.

Tomkins had been terribly avenged.

After a time the Chinaman went away, leaving the corpse of Cesare Iannotto dangling, the bloody bits of what had been Big Tommy still on the floor where they had fallen.

Somebody turned out the lights. The cavern was dark.

We waited, silent.

At last I whispered, "I've got to get out of here."

I think Derek figured I was going to have hysterics. His hand patted my shoulder, he whispered, "Of course, ducks. Let me go first."

We walked through pitch blackness for a few steps, then he turned on his flashlight beam. The white light cut through the darkness, showed us the little opening that was the tunnel mouth. We went for it without stopping to look around us.

It was night when we came out into the fresh sea air. We both stopped, pausing on the rock ledge, hunting for the rope we'd left there. It was gone. Derek said, "How do we get up there now?"

"I climb," I muttered.

He braced himself, he leaned against the rock cliff while I clambered onto his shoulders. Derek is a tall man, so by standing on top of him, I could reach a bush growing into a crack between two rocks. My hand tightened on it, very gingerly I hauled myself up. At any second I expected to pull the bush out by its roots and go plunging over the ledge onto the rocks far below, where the waves pounded into froth.

The bush held. I got a toe in a rock crack, stood and reached upward. This time my hand went around a rock. I pulled myself toward it.

I was sobbing, exhausted, but I could see the rim of the cliff above me. I was so close to it! I stretched on tiptoe, but my fingertips only brushed against it. My eyes looked around me. There was no other handhold.

"Derek," I breathed. "I'm stuck."

He was about ten feet below me, helpless to do more than stare up at me in mute agony. "Can you climb down?" he called.

I knew I couldn't. I could never find that bush, that crack between the rocks on the downward path. I leaned my head against the cold stone and let the tears ooze from my eyes.

Then a face came over the rim.

I found myself staring up into the moonface of our guide.

"What are you doing?" he gasped.

"Help me, help me," I whimpered.

"You wait," he called, and ran.

He was back with a rope that he fastened around a treetrunk and dropped over the edge of the cliff. I put my hands on it, but I was too weak to pull myself up. I'd been down to hell and back, and I was feeling the reaction.

I felt the rope tighten. Behind and below me, Derek was starting his climb. I knew the touch of his hand on my ankle, on my calf.

"Sit on my shoulder, pet," he said.

I let my rump find his broad shoulder, felt myself boosted upward as he used his hands on the rope, pulling us both up. Then our guide had hold of me, and was drawing me over the edge of the cliff. I fell on the ground and lay there.

Derek came up over the rim under his own power. I heard him muttering to the guide, something about our taking a little walk and getting lost. The guide was furious with us both, but he was also relieved. I guess he was afraid of what might happen to him if the authorities learned we'd been away from him for such a long period of time.

"I fall asleep," he growled.

"I know. It was such a nice day, we had to take a stroll. We went further than we expected, and for a lark we started down the cliff. We fell but weren't hurt."

"We go back now. Long overstay, here."

Derek lifted me to my feet. I leaned against him as we beat feet toward the Shanghai sedan. Our guide fussed beside us, every step of the way.

He said, as he opened the rear door for me, "1 will drive, you two will just sit there. And it might be better not to say you went off by yourselves. It will only make the authorities suspicious."

I thought that was an excellent idea, and said so. "We will not even mention that you fell asleep. We will say the car broke down on the road, and that it took a long time to fix it, if anything is said."

The guide looked happy, nodding his head.

In the darkness of the back seat I fumbled at the cameras. I found a Graflex, and after sliding the jewels from my pocket, wrapped inside my handkerchief, hid them inside it. At least, I was clean.

When we were back in the private house overlooking Lake Tai, it was Derek's turn to unload his jewels. We stuffed them tightly inside the Graflex, removing the film, and said mutual prayers that nobody would open the camera from here on in.

As we were getting dressed for dinner, I wandered into Derek's room to have him zip me up. While the tab was sliding up my back, I asked, "1 wonder how come those tong men didn't disturb the guide? They must have seen him sleeping."

"Ducks, they don't want to make waves. Even if they'd killed the poor slob and dumped his body into the sea, there would have been an investigation."

"Won't there be an investigation about the Mafia boys?"

He grinned. "There will, as soon as I'm in Hong Kong. I intend writing Wing Dock a letter, telling him about that cave. His 'discovery' of it—probably he'll wait until the tong boys are having a meeting—will make him a big hero in Red China. He'll be given an important post, he'll get a decoration of some sort. All of which will make him very friendly toward me."

I arched a stare at him. "Do you realize I haven't taken one single picture with that compact camera you gave me? We haven't been allowed off limits, not even once. We-ell, except for that time we spent in the cave."

"Changed my mind about that. Since I'll be in so good with Wing Dock and the Red Chinese, I've decided not to rock the boat by publishing anything they'll scowl at. I can make enough money from a regular picture book without doublecrossing our guests."

"Not to mention the Tears of Kouan-in and the Eggs of Chi Nong and the Ch'u nu pearl."

"I'll give a diamond and an emerald to Kim Chow. That will keep him happy. What would you like, pet?"

"A diamond, I guess. I'll leave it to you."

"Well, your job is done. Your Mafia buttons are dead. I figure we'll spend another two weeks here and there making more snapshots, then board a plane to home territory."

"Suits me fine," I laughed.

His eyes ran over my body in a clinging cheong-sam of black silk I'd picked up in Soochow while on one of our photography trips. I was naked under it, he saw the imprint of my breasts and upper thighs, my small belly. He licked his lips.

"Ducks, what say we hold a sort of celebration tonight in your room, over a bottle of rice wine? The house is private, I'm sure nobody will be checking on us. We'll have ourselves a ball."

I patted him where he was starting to grow.

"Sounds nice. Tell me more over dinner."

Arm in arm, we started for the staircase.

TO THE READER

If you enjoyed this book, you will be glad to know that there are many others just as well written, just as interesting, to be had in the Fiction House Press Library.

You will find the Fiction House Press Library online at

www.FictionHousePress.com

www.ingramcontent.com/pod-product-compliance
Lightning Source LLC
Chambersburg PA
CBHW060400030726
47497CB00003B/795